THE THAI WIFE STORY
JOY

THE THAI WIFE SERIES OF NOVELS

BOOK 1

THE THAI WIFE STORY

JOY

THE THAI WIFE SERIES OF NOVELS

BOOK 1

BY

RAYMOND GREENLAW

ROXY PUBLISHING, LLC
CAPE CORAL, FLORIDA
UNITED STATES OF AMERICA

COPY EDITOR—Marjorie Roxburgh
COVER DESIGN—Robert Greenlaw, Jr.
TEXT DESIGN—Raymond Greenlaw
PHOTOGRAPHER—Raymond Greenlaw
TYPESETTING—Raymond Greenlaw

ROXY PUBLISHING, LLC
Cape Coral, Florida
United States of America

http://drraymondgreenlaw.com
First edition, paperback.
Book 1 in *The Thai Wife Series of Novels*.

The Thai Wife Story Joy is a work of fiction. All con-
tents in the book are either the product of the author's imagination or are used fictitiously. Any resemblance of the main characters to actual persons
is purely coincidental.

ISBN 978-1-947467-20-0 (Paperback)

DEDICATION

Joy, thanks for introducing me to Thailand.

PREFACE

THE INSPIRATIONS for these novels are the beautiful and friendly women of Thailand. This is book 1 of the series. The main characters are fictitious, and any resemblance to actual persons is purely coincidental. Parts are historical fiction. No linkage between the events described and the policies of any nation state should be drawn. The author possesses a deep love for Thailand, and no part should be interpreted as otherwise. These novels are storytelling, written for reader enjoyment.

The books in *The Thai Wife Series of Novels* use a phonetic-Thai spelling. There are many different ways of writing Thai words in English, and my method is but one of them. For the most part, I don't worry about exact pronunciations and tones. Any foreigner who speaks Thai will recognize the intended Thai words from my phonetic spellings.

I include a Thai-to-English dictionary in an appendix, so you can look up the meaning of any Thai word contained in this book. Anyone interested in learning more about the Thai language can obtain a copy of my book, *Essential Conversational Thai,* co-authored with Saowaluk Rattanaudomsawat.

There are times in the text when several people are speaking or making sounds simultaneously. I indicate this by identifying the character who is speaking followed by an arrow (→). For example,

Tom → "Hello."

Joy → "Sa waa dii ka."

signifies that Tom said, 'Hello,' at the exact same time as Joy said, 'Sa waa dii ka.' The spatial order of these two lines is not significant. So,

Joy → "Sa waa dii ka."

Tom → "Hello."

has an identical meaning.

I've expressed a Thai person speaking imperfect English in an authentic fashion by including the usual grammatical errors, omitted words, and common mispronunciations. Those readers who have traveled in Thailand will recognize these solecisms immediately. I've established a YouTube channel, called *Raymond Greenlaw's Writings*, where you can listen to me reading chapters of the book.

The novels are intended for mature audiences. Although several characters in the story engage in unsafe sex, the author advises against this. I hope you'll enjoy reading this series of novels, as much as I enjoyed writing it. This series was researched and written over a period of 15 years.

Although I've tried to be as careful as possible in my writing, a few grammatical errors and typos may remain. I apologize in advance. I would like to eliminate any errors in future editions of this work. I appreciate any corrections.

Raymond Greenlaw
July 26, 2021
Last edited: May 2, 2023

ACKNOWLEGMENTS

A SPECIAL THANKS to Wongduean Boh-thong for her support and encouragement, for her work with our cover model, and for her belief that eventually I would finish the first book in the series. Thanks to Aom for modeling.

A warm thanks to Marjorie Roxburgh for her edits and improvements. Thanks to Paul and Helen Göransson for their suggestions. Thanks to my nephew, Robert Greenlaw, Jr., for assisting with the cover design and setting up my YouTube channel. Thanks to my mentor, Adrian Plante, for his continued support throughout the last 45+ years.

A sincere thanks to all reviewers and early readers, both farangs and Thais, who provided me with constructive comments. Your suggestions have helped me to improve this novel, and they will help me with other novels in the series too. I'm indebted to you. Many others have contributed to this project, and a big thanks goes out to you all.

CHAPTER 1

I WAIT IN MY chair. Although I haven't started my prestigious position, I'm going to ask for a one-year leave of absence. I'm hopeful. The COVID-19 pandemic, my findings on the laptop, and the all-consuming editing … I need time. I simply need more time.

"Come please, him Dean see you now," the young woman said in a captivating Asian accent.

She separates me from my thoughts. I don't mind her mistakes at all. She is lovely. I walk past a wall sign that reads 'Office of the Academic Dean and Provost of the United States Naval Academy.'

"Hi, there. Sorry to keep you."

Due to social-distancing rules, the Dean and I don't shake hands. Instead, we exchange nods and smiles. I sit ten feet away, where either he or his delightful assistant positioned a chair.

"No problem at all."

"Well, what can I do for you?"

The Dean has a reputation for being professional, thoughtful, and supportive. He is a straightforward guy—he does what he feels is in the best interests of the Naval Academy, his faculty and staff, and the Midshipmen. I accepted my new post based largely on his abilities and enthusiasm. He's doing a great job handling the pandemic. I don't beat around the bush.

"Dean, I've come to request a one-year sabbatical. I need time to pursue an unfinished project. It's been a crazy year."

I don't feel it's necessary to elaborate any further. We know sabbaticals come only after six years. The coronavirus alters everything. He's quick thinking. He sees I've made up my mind. People at his level in the DOD are trained to make decisions. They've earned the right to trust their instincts.

"As you're no doubt aware, two of our alumni, the brilliant scientist, Albert Michelson, and the world-peace advocate, President Jimmy Carter, received Nobel Prizes. Michelson taught here for four years after graduation. Later, he won the Nobel in physics. You're the first who comes with the credential of a Nobel. Having a laureate in literature, well, I'm sure you know what that means for the institution, and the impact you can have on our English Department."

The Dean's expression conveys a clear meaning. Before my signing, we discussed the shortcomings of the program. He leans forward at my comprehension. I feel a sense of duty to my country. I'll be proud to educate our future leaders. The Dean breaks into a smile. I can see he's made up his mind.

"We'll put out a press release shortly about the delay in your starting. In these times, it won't cause a stir. Everyone will be disappointed, but no one more than I. And, when you're ready and things have settled down, we'll get you in here, just as fast as we can. It'll be a true pleasure to have you working at the Academy. I'll let the superintendent know."

I gesture thanks. There isn't much to add. As a Nobel laureate, I have an unfair advantage. The coronavirus worries me. The Dean understands my concern. I stand up.

"Give my regards to the Sup. Thanks, Dean."

"In a week or so, Miss Nguyen will send you a packet to process your leave and continuation. It'll clarify a new starting date. If you have any questions, don't hesitate to contact her. She's real hands on. We'll be in touch. Good luck with your project. Can't wait to learn more."

"Okay. Thanks again."

"Bye."

"Good-bye."

As I exit the Dean's office, I notice two identical, hand-crafted, exquisite lacquer liquor cabinets with bright-orange goldfish paintings, covering their entire sprinkled with gold-glitter surfaces. The aquatic masterpieces with their flowing fins and breezy tails radiate and gleam magnificently, as the light penetrating the windows brings them to life. While walking past, the varying angle of the reflecting light causes the fish to swim and splash about in their shiny ponds. I admire the genius of the artist.

The relics bringing the goldfish to life appear Vietnamese, and I can't help but wonder if they aren't connected to Miss Nguyen. I smile uninhibitedly. She reciprocates. Her smile is one that you want to frame and hang above your headboard, so on lonely nights, you can tip your head back and be with her. A glance at her features resets my brain like an Etch-A-Sketch being readied for a drawing. With a pleasantly blank mind, I head for the door.

I smile again, at no one in particular, and walk out of Nimitz Hall, taking far-larger steps than when I first entered the building. I'm energized. My project will get my full attention. I thank the Dean, and I thank the beautiful Miss Nguyen too. My cheeks stretch with excitement.

As I advance past Rickover Hall, I punch my fist in the air. I repeat the salute when I pass Michelson. My passion is what the Swedish Academy rewarded in my earlier works—*The Thai Boy and His Evolving Kingdom, Please Don't Thai Me Down,* and *The Scorpion Girl from Issarn.*

When Bob Dylan won his Nobel, he was twice my age. I accepted my award in Stockholm and broke Rudyard Kipling's record, as the youngest recipient ever. I possess a deep sense of self-worth that is more linked to my parents' acceptance and approval than the Nobel's. My folks want me to keep writing, but they're proud of me for accepting the teaching position at the Naval Academy.

I stride across the near-deserted Yard over to Stockdale's statue and read its frontal inscription, which is a quote from Sir Winston Churchill. I walk around. The quotation on the side panel begins, "As senior prisoner of war in Vietnam from 1965 to 1973 ..." I look up and stare at the Severn River, and the bobbing masts of the Naval Academy's boats.

In some strange way, I know my walk to this statue is linked to Miss Nguyen. She reminds me of a Vietnamese girl whom I met in Bangkok many years earlier. Like the budding seamen sailing in front of me, I find myself gliding through the soft currents of the Perfume River with the Vietnamese beauty.

CHAPTER 2

BACK AT my Tecumseh apartment, I pour my-self a strong one. From my fourth-floor window, looking out across Spa Creek beyond the marinas, I see the top of the Naval Academy's Chapel. I stare. I wonder where Miss Nguyen is. I wonder what she's doing. I swish a swig around in my mouth and lean back. As I swallow, gravity assists. A narcissistic feeling washes over me.

I'm proud of myself and what I've accomplished, but I feel stupid for feeling that way. I know that in getting back to my writing, I'll quickly be humbled. Although people think I'm a natural, I often struggle to find the right words. Non-writers don't understand the difficulty in producing a quality sentence, and everyone is a critic. In a one-minute rant, an unqualified pompous ass can slam two years of careful work.

The damned coronavirus makes my life topsy-turvy. It forces me to rethink a number of assumptions. But, what prompted me to go meet with the Dean is this mysterious laptop. I discovered it a few weeks earlier. For your information, completeness, and accuracy, I recount the events leading up to the Dean's meeting.

***

I found the dusty laptop beneath a pile of stuff in my rented apartment. There were copies of *The Hunt for Red October* and *Patriot Games* in the mix. Scribbled inside both drafts, I saw edits. Tom Clancy spent time in Annapolis. Although I know that Tom used a penthouse at the Ritz-Carlton Residences in Baltimore as his primary domicile, I didn't know if he'd ever resided at the Tecumseh. I wasn't going to poke around asking questions about a famous dead man, especially during a pandemic.

When I turned on the laptop, its battery was dead. I had no idea how long it'd been submerged in that pile, but I felt a little stupid. Down on my knees, pawing through the rat's nest, a fleeing cockroach scared the bejeebers out of me. I recovered and picked up a post-it note. As I started to crumple the yellow square, I noticed writing. On comparison, I saw it's in the same hand as used to edit Clancy's manuscripts.

The writing is from one of my-favorite poems by Robert Frost. When I squinted, I felt a tsunami of alcohol breaking against my forehead. I heard a sea retreating and regained my balance. I drank too much. I blame my drinking on the pandemic.

I read aloud, "And miles to go before I sleep, RF, 1922." I recognized the verse from "Stopping by Woods on a Snowy Evening." I searched through the jumble and located a power cable. After pulling the dust bunnies off the prongs, I plugged in. A green light flickered; a red one flashed in my brain.

When I saw that Windows was loading, I had time to fix another drink. I then moved to the dining-room table. Windows prompted me for a password. To meet requirements, I form passwords by extracting the first symbol of each word in an easy-to-remember phrase. I can't manage unnatural combinations of symbols. Having Frost's quote, I gave it a try.

I typed in 'AmtgbIs, RF, 1922.' With trepidation, I hit enter. I watched; I waited; it worked.

"Clancy, you're a genius!"

I grabbed the table to prevent a fall. I printed the password on a post-it note. I added '2 spaces' and '2 commas' to prevent confusion. I stuck the note on the cover. My palms were sweaty. In my paranoia, I scanned the room to see if anyone was watching me. Of course, no one was. I was alone.

On the Desktop, the folder labeled Thai-WifeNovels stood out. I opened it. Inside were ten folders. They were nicknames of Thai women. I clicked on Joy. There were dozens of files. I double clicked JoyPart1. While Windows opened the WORD document, I grabbed the bottle of Maker's Mark.

I was drunk and tired, but something told me to do more. Sleep tugged at me, but I fought. My phone rang; I ignored it. I began reading …

CHAPTER 3

EVEN THE EARLY November temperatures in Bangkok fried my brain. Rivulets ran into the corners of my mouth. A sideways swipe stopped the salt from burning my eyes.

His intro brought back vivid memories of Thailand's brutally hot climate. I hadn't been in Bangkok for a while, but one doesn't easily forget being boiled alive. The author likes alliteration. What had I stumbled on? I battled my fatigue. I continued.

Thoughts of Afghanistan, Somalia, and Iraq invaded my mind. Bangkok punched me in the face with a left-and-right combination of heat and humidity. Bad memories induced cranial vomiting of undigested events. I walked fast, then faster. My thoughts kept up.

The fetid sois, oodles of street hawkers, and throngs of tourists couldn't wrench me away. "Stay calm and focused." I fought against my demons. "Keep walking." I wanted an ice-cold drink from 7-

11. Panic attack. Hurried shallow breathing. The feeling of being caught in a trap. "Shit."

"Hey, Mister!"

I lowered my hands. My eyes scanned. Her voice returned me to the streets. My heart rate slowed. In the discombobulated collage, only after hearing her voice, did I notice the tuk-tuks, horns, jackhammers, and buses. The noise avalanche triggered by 'mister' slammed into my ears. I wanted to hear her again. I wasn't in Annapolis anymore.

I laughed. No, but I am. After a generous gulp of Maker's, I continued.

Just across Sukhumvit Road from Nana Plaza Soi 4, I could see a 7-11. I egged myself on, "Don't let Bangkok win." I heard the seductive voice again.

"Hey, Mister! Welcome."

The call was close. It wasn't really a call. It was a sweet whisper/request. My curiosity defeated my thirst. I slowed. I stopped.

The author's description of Bangkok's punishing weather made me thirsty too. I took a drink. I wiped my brow.

I wasn't sure if I was her target. I painted a canvas of a tan, young Thai girl with Caravaggio-red lips. My mood changed. Funny, the heat no longer troubled me.

"Hey, Mister! Handsome man. Massage ka?"

I felt a tiny hand squeezing mine, as an out-of-breath little Thai girl arrived. Her touch felt good.

She caught me. Bangkok freed me of other concerns and broke my chains of panic. I squeezed back. My eyes met her irresistible Thai smile.

"You good smile, Mister. Blue eye ka."

The Thai doll squeezed my hand again. I squeezed back. I bit Lolita's red lipstick, white teeth, cleavage, short skirt, sexy heels, and innocent-smile bait. When I squeezed under my-own initiative this time, it spoke volumes. I hadn't said one word though.

"You need massage with Joy? You handsome man ka. Wery handsome ka."

I stared at the desirable teenager. I wondered if 'with joy' is a Sukhumvit-street code. On returning from Asia, my SEAL buddies told me tales of happy endings. The girl casually tossed her waist-length hair behind. When she flashed her white teeth again, I returned her smile. She reached up and touched my parched lips, as if trying to extract reassuring words. The magic potion of her Thai smile created physical needs.

Intoxicated on her brew, I opened my wandering mouth and blurted out, "Yes. Yes, I do. I do."

The magician smiled. I laughed. I imagined a priest popping the big question, "Tom, do you take this girl to be your lawfully wedded wife?" I responded, "Yes, I do. I do." I came to Thailand to fulfill two missions: the first involved serving my country, and the second involved finding a Thai wife. I nearly chalked up the latter one.

The girl could interpret my actions instantly. I couldn't hide information from her; I couldn't encrypt my demeanor. She turned me into a puppet. Once her concoction took over, logic vanished. I loved her jaunty smile.

"Me good ka. Good service. You li-eh?"

"Yes, I like. I like very much."

I fought against the word 'love.'

"You wery handsome ka."

"Thanks. You're very pretty."

"Come, Mister."

She took my hand and led me away, to I didn't know where. I didn't care where, and I followed. I wondered where the tuk-tuks, motorcycles, taxis, and buses had gone, the terrible smells, and the annoying hawkers. She made them disappear. The city block became our own, private steam room. We walked spritely. I wanted to run.

"This way, Mister."

"Okay," I responded after a mesmerizing delay. "How old are you?"

"Sixteen ka."

"Oh."

"Ka."

She was only 16. The age of majority in Thailand is 15. Although a one-year buffer existed in my favor, in a matter of minutes, she and Bangkok managed to flip my moral compass. If she'd said 14, I would have gone along.

As we negotiated the crowded soi, I followed behind. The heels accentuated her sexy calf muscles. Her curved hips swayed back and forth rhythmically, and I wondered if she was full grown. Even with the stilettos, she only reached my shoulder. I stared at the straps binding her ankles.

I reassured her periodic backward glances that I was in tow. Was she thinking about finding a husband to take care of her and her family? Little mattered to me. My mind—manipulated by the ingredients that she had tossed into and stirred within my body's cauldron—possessed a solitary thought.

"Mister, my name Joy ka. You? You name, Mister?"

When I realized that 'with joy' wasn't a street code, I felt like a fool. She is as innocent as she seemed. I credited Bangkok with my emotional and moral tides. I coached myself. "Relax, Tom. Take it easy."

I paused, took a sip, and scratched the top of my head. Tom? Only when I read the main-character's name again, did something click. In his earlier writings, I heard Tom Clancy used his first name for the protagonist's, until he settled on a name. He was familiar with Navy SEALs, nautical jargon, and Thailand. I took a long swig, praying the alcohol would bring me answers and energy, but instead, it sabotaged any remaining rationality and will power.

Feeling exhausted, I decided to print out the material. I would take it to bed with me. I wanted to keep reading.

CHAPTER 4

I WOKE UP HUNG over, which during these depressing times, is a frequent occurrence. After splashing cold water on my face, I picked up the printer's output and tossed it on the table. It was only then I realized I'd passed out the night before.

I boiled water. A couple minutes later, I found the ginger tea. I booted up the laptop. While Windows loaded, I thumbed through the hardcopy. A few questions came to mind. Would readers know there are thousands of 7-11s in Thailand? That a tuk-tuk is a three-wheeled taxi? About Caravaggio's intense realism? Nabokov's writing?

I think Joy is from Northeast Thailand (Issarn). She probably has financial obligations—debts accumulated by parents and family members. Many Issarn farm girls become sex workers in Bangkok, Pattaya, and Phuket. When American soldiers took R&R during the Vietnam War, the bargirl scene started. The phrases 'short time' and 'long time' and 'me love you long time' originated there. I suppose Soi Cowboy wouldn't exist, if not for Americans.

Attractive young girls are sold by their parents to pay off gambling debts. Thais love to gamble. Issarn girls search for foreign men to marry. Many uneducated Thais view foreigners as ATMs. Marrying means becoming rich, not just for them, but the extended family too.

Not long ago, the wage for a 12-hour workday in Thailand was raised from two to eight dollars, whereas a bargirl can earn 30 dollars per hour. A girl can earn nearly 50 times as much by providing intimate services. For many, this wage gap is too big to ignore.

The lifestyle that a bargirl leads—dressing up, partying, dating rich men, and receiving gifts—appeals to some Thai girls. The money helps and motivates. I heard it said, "You can take the girl out of the bar, but you can't take the bar out of the girl."

On my trips to Thailand, I chatted with bargirls and did research on them for my books. In most bars, the girls can decide whether or not they want to leave with a customer, short time or long time. So, if a customer is distasteful, she can wait for a better prospect.

Although some Thai bargirls are innocent, others are savvy well beyond their years. They learn how to manipulate men at an early age. I collected a Nobel Prize in literature for writing about Thailand's bargirls. I know them. I miss Bangkok. I looked out my window at the Naval Academy's Chapel and stared.

I sipped my ginger tea. This guy is a good writer. I can make him better. After adding handwritten notes to the manuscript, I put it aside. I opened Joy-Part3. I returned to where Joy asked Tom his name.

CHAPTER 5

I SAID, "HAPPY to meet you, Joy."
I hesitated. I considered providing my real name, but even in my infatuated state, I couldn't be that stupid. I regained my composure and invented a title and nickname.

"Call me Doctor Adventure. People call me Doc, for short."

And just like that, I gave myself a new credential and moniker in Thailand. The name marked the start of another beginning.

"Oh, you big man ka. You doctor?"

"Yes."

"You smart man. You wery big man ka. Big muscle too. Wery handsome ka. He, he, he."

"Thanks, Joy. You're beautiful."

"Thin' so? You sweet mouth ka."

"Thanks."

"Ka."

Joy and I still held hands. We passed an Indian tailor's shop, an hourly hotel with an Arab proprietor, a Western-style restaurant, two Thai freelancers, a youth hostel, a McDonald's, a man selling insect snacks, a spa, a Thai restaurant, a Swiss hotel, a panhandler with one leg, a woman selling mangoes, a shoe-shine boy, a dress shop, a man carelessly splitting open coconuts with a yellow meat cleaver, a multi-colored and worn umbrella protecting fried chicken, a rusty fruit cart, a girl mixing shakes, a smelly durian stall, a half-dozen motorcycle taxi drivers, a gold shop, a pharmacy, a frail biddy selling ice cream, a beggar drinking from a poorly hidden bottle, a laundromat, a shoe shop, a music store, and a guy in military fatigues selling army trinkets. Tourists of many nationalities walked past.

Joy's silky hair revealed a shapely orb on each pendulum swing. It hypnotized me. I admired. Bangkok planted thoughts in my head.

"Here, Doc."

Joy turned and smiled. One clump of her hair stuck together, taking the shape of a black asp. I read the peeling inscription over the door.

"Lollipop Two?"

Joy tipped her head sideways, resulting in a serpentine movement of the hair clump.

"No Lollipop ka. Change owner. Sell ka. Now Lucky Massage. Lucky. He, he, he. Wery lucky."

At the sliding-glass door, Joy flicked off her heels.

"Leave shoe here ka."

"Okay."

"Ka."

While removing my shoes, I bent over where I got a close-up of Joy's feet. Her toenails were pedicured into triangular points, similar to a lady's fingernails. Her cuticles were pressed back, to elongate her toenails. Each one is a third as long as its toe. Her feet are mirror images. I admired and stared, dreaming. When she brushed a stiletto into position—using her well-balanced foot—my fantasizing continued.

Joy's toes formed bright-red staircases. From the big toe down, each is shorter by the exact-same amount. Her toes are flawlessly shaped and symmetrical. The lengths are perfect. The olive-colored skin on her feet and ankles contrasted the glossy-enameled toenails.

The four, tiny, and tapered gaps separating her toes are the same width, when considering the gaps at the same distance away from her foot. The identical, knife-like endpoints rested on linear toes. I wanted a gigantic oil painting of her feet and ankles—bound in black-strapped stilettos—for my gym.

I slapped myself on the leg. I took a pull on my lukewarm tea, which was too cold to enjoy. I didn't want to stop reading, so I pushed the cup aside. Windows popped up its low-battery warning, and I plugged in the charging cable. I decided to heat up more water.

Chapter 6

WITH A FRESH CUP *of ginger tea, I started reading from a brighter screen.*

As I straightened up from adding my shoes to the pile, I caught Joy staring. I smiled. She raised her hand to her mouth and giggled. I followed her eyes which seemed to say, "I did something wrong, didn't I?"

A licentious urge to punish Joy welled up inside. She controlled me. I realized that my life was about to change. I was helpless and would do whatever she wanted.

"God dammit, Tom!" I witnessed this behavior and its outcome way-too-many times, with gullible foreign men getting their hearts broken by girls half their age. Along with their hearts, men had their life savings stolen too. I hoped that Tom wouldn't get burned.

My trainers looked out of place in the pile of women's sexy footwear. Joy's shoes had the highest heels. On the window, I saw a picture of a foot with pressure points labeled. A sign read, 'Foot Masage, Thai Masage, Oil Masage,' and displayed durations and pricings. The repeated misspelling of 'massage' lightened my mood. With Joy leading me, we entered.

I found myself barking orders at my screen. I laughed at my behavior. I was hungry, but I wanted to see how the massage turned out.

"Hi everyone. Sa waa dii krap."

I grinned smugly, as a large number of masseuses and a cool blast from the air conditioner greeted me. Joy smiled proudly. While she solicited business, other girls hoped something would just fall in their laps. They looked up from their mobiles.

A lovely masseuse → "Sa waa dii ka."

Shop girl 1 → "Joy, you lucky girl."

"Him big man."

"Good shape ka."

"Ha-low. Ha-low, Mister."

I said → "Hi. Hello."

Shop girl 2 → "Strong and handsome man ka."

Shop girl 3 → "Him muscle man. Blue eye ka."

"Ka."

"Mister, you need two girl. Ha, ha, ha …"

Shop girl 1 → "Oil massage ka."

Shop girl 4 → "Farang wery rich."

"Oil good. Mai pang."

"Chorp ka."

They spoke to us in rapid succession. I felt as if they'd been waiting there all day to greet us. The girls thought I was rich. Joy watched them. I surveyed the room. Some girls spoke in a language I didn't recognize. It wasn't Thai.

"He, he, he."

"Him wery strong."

"Good shape ka. Weally wery good shape."

"Look muscle him, Aom."

"Ka. I look ka. Wery good shape ka. I look."

"Ka."

Joy beamed. I saw many jealous stares. They fueled her ego. As we went past holding hands, several masseuses teased Joy. She tightened her grip. I heard silly giggling.

//Unfinished, edit until end note.

The girls believed that Joy was going to earn an extra 500 baht for giving her customer a special massage. A strong man would finish quickly. She would wipe up, excuse herself, secretly throw away the soiled tissue, wash her hands, and return to his massage, as if nothing unusual had happened.

If she liked her customer, she would watch. If not, her hand would become a piston—moving up and down in identical strokes, without feeling or conviction—while her idle fingers tapped. The girls gladly would have traded positions with Joy—both for the money and the opportunity to be with a rich farang. He might be single.

Notes about previous section.

Mention there are 30 to 40 baht in a dollar over the time that the series spans. Tom wouldn't have all this information yet, so it can't be written from his point of view.

//End note. End of material to edit. TC

There is my answer. The manuscript is unfinished, and TC intended to come back and rewrite these few paragraphs, and maybe other parts too. In the habit of printing the files, I located this passage and scribbled a few margin notes about how I planned to finish it. I'll return here later. I intend to clean up draft sections.

CHAPTER 7

THE DAYS FLEW past. I was doing more editing than reading. As a Nobel laureate, I feel an obligation to improve the manuscript. I reviewed the first part many times. Occasionally, I deleted a passage or toned down the language. But, at other times, I spiced things up.

Over the previous week, I poked around in the folders. I confirmed the author planned a series of novels about Thai women. The subfolders are named: Joy, Star, Sugar, Gun, Patty, Opal, Apple, Peach, Moon, and Ying. I saw that the Joy folder contains a complete book.

On delving deeper, I learned that each folder contains an entire book draft. There are hundreds of files. The Peach folder alone contains several dozen files. When I started reading those, I learned that Peach is a flirtatious major in the Thai army.

Each time I read a story, I found myself captivated. Although needing polishing, these works should be published. They give information about Thailand, its sex industry, Navy SEALs, covert operations, cyber-attacks, and more. The tales are also love stories about a man searching for a Thai wife.

Being confined alters my thinking. I feel a duty to finish these works. The author was ambitious. I estimate I'll be editing 2,500 pages. Given my knowledge of Thailand, bargirl experiences, and writing skills, I'm the person to complete these works. I discovered this treasure trove for some reason. I feel the need to complete it.

I only recently committed to accepting a Distinguished Professorship in the English Department at the United States Naval Academy. If I devote one month to each book, I'll need about one year to finish. I'll have some explaining to do with publishers. I'm not sure I can list my name on the cover, as the primary author. Being a Nobel laureate, the publisher will want that.

Publishers want to sell books and make money. They're not concerned about the quality of writing per se, only that they maximize profits. We'll need to discuss the original author's role. His estate will want him listed as a co-author, but I'm getting ahead of myself.

When I interviewed months ago, the Dean and I got along great. He convinced me that they need me. And, he feels I'll derive great satisfaction from working with Midshipmen and serving my country.

My parents are proud of me. My father distinguished himself in Vietnam. Because I accepted the position at the Academy, I faced a real dilemma.

The obvious choice was to meet with the Dean and simply request a leave. When he finds out how important this project is to me and how passionate I feel about it, I believe he'll be sympathetic. With the pandemic, many people's lives are impacted drastically.

Prompted by my obsession with the manuscripts, I made up my mind to request a one-year leave. I called the Dean's Office and set up an appointment. As the date of my meeting approaches, I continue to make excellent progress on *The Thai Wife Series of Novels*. I know a sabbatical is the only way forward.

***

Earlier, I relayed the news that the Dean granted me a sabbatical. I'm expecting to hear from the Dean's Office and Miss Nguyen any day. I'm sure there will be lots of paperwork. I wonder if Miss Nguyen will deliver the materials. Now that you're caught up, let's return to Lucky Massage.

CHAPTER 8

WHEN I ENTERED Lucky Massage, the tallest girl stared at me. Later, I would learn her name is Bpee. Even from a sitting position, her statuesque frame dominates that of the other girls. She has a beautiful face, conspicuous breasts, light-colored skin, a pointed nose, and toned muscles. Her demeanor is more aggressive than the others, and her body more mature and stronger.

When Bpee noticed I was checking her out, she climbed onto stage. She performed a three-act play starring her tongue, promiscuous red lips, and fingers. The performance culminated when she swallowed and licked her fingers. Her audacious display stated that she wanted to perform fellatio on me right there, with the girls comprising a voyeuristic gallery. Bpee planted the thoughts that she intended to in my brain.

Joy led me away from Bpee's entertaining performance and my fantasies. We went up a steep set of stairs, illuminated by just one long, flickering fluorescent bulb. The stairway smells musty, and the concrete stairs are uneven. We entered a dimly lit and windowless room. I inhaled and the incense gave me a buzz. We bumped. When she giggled, I knew she felt me.

I half-heartedly listened to the spa music that was being piped into the prison-cell-sized room. The music drowned out external noise. Although the small room contains just a mattress on the floor, the modest setting mattered little. Delightful Joy squeezed my hand and gently released. A silly giggle followed.

"Take all clothes off ka. Joy came back soon. He, he, he."

"Okay."

"Ka."

When Joy opened the door, I scanned the room. I pulled the sticky T-shirt over my head and draped it on a hook. I removed my shorts. I placed my underwear on a second pin and positioned my shorts there. My baseball cap went on top. I stuffed my watch in my shorts, alongside my mobile. I removed my wallet from the opposite pocket, and counted.

My wallet contained 17,800 baht. I put the wallet back and stretched out on the thin mattress. The sheet smelled recently laundered. I was thankful. I felt remorse at my distrust in Joy, but I'd heard horror stories from others. Just as I awkwardly began pulling the sheet over, Joy entered. She dead bolted the door.

"Joy back ka. Ready, Doc?"

"Yes, I'm ready."

"He, he, he."

My hunger gets the best of me. The Tecumseh is across the street from two of the best steakhouses in the region. I toss a coin and decide on Lewnes' Steak House. They've been around since 1921. The next time, I'll place my order at Ruth's Chris Steak House. They can walk my meal over quickly.

CHAPTER 9

GOOSE BUMPS AROSE everywhere on Tom's body, as the young Thai masseuse salaciously dragged the sheet across him. From her kneeling position, Joy cast it aside. Aroused by touching her customer, she circled three fingers on herself. While looking down at his V-shaped back, she pressed with resolve and exhaled forcefully. After her all-too-brief digression, she returned to him.

She noticed a tattoo between his upper arm and shoulder—the skeleton frog that most green-faced men tattooed somewhere. There is no writing on it, but Joy couldn't read anyway.

"You frog tattoo?"

"Yes."

"Joy li-eh."

"Thanks."

"Ka."

The teenager placed a bottle of oil beside Tom's head. She climbed onto his lumbar region and began rubbing his shoulders. She could feel the moisture between her legs. Joy pressed her knees firmly into his back. She balanced herself easily.

Tom guessed Joy weighed 80 pounds. As she massaged his shoulders, she shifted her knees and body weight to massage his lower back. He felt happy with Joy on top—a situation he wasn't accustomed to. He noticed an increase in her breathing, but missed that she was close to orgasming. To distract herself, she began talking.

"Joy not speak English no good. Me no study. No money study."

"I understand you, Joy. Your English is fine. Much better than my Thai."

"He, he, he. No, me English not good ka. Me no money study. You good man. Where from, Doc?"

"I'm from the U-S-A."

"Wery good. You America."

"Yes, I'm American. I live in Maryland."

"Merry ..."

"Maryland."

"Merry wan? See, me say you, me speak English not good."

"You're fine. Yes, near Washington, DC."

"Ka."

Joy had never heard of Washington, DC.

While they chatted, she continued massaging. Tom felt comfortable with her touch. Despite the language barrier, their communication flowed. Although the massage had only started, he hoped she would roll him over soon. That thought became an obsession.

"Joy li-eh America. America man good. Vegas, San Fran, and L-A ka. Thai man no good. Him drink too much. Him drink whiskey ka. Thai whiskey too much. Him no good. Joy not li-eh."

"I drink too much," Tom confessed.

Yeah, me too. I reach the end of the file and save it. I wonder why it ended here. In anticipation, I open the next file, JoyPart5. I'm relieved to see the story continues from where it left off.

Although I'm enjoying the narrative, I realize the book is only in draft form. In this chapter, the narration switches to third person. It works for me. I want to know more about what Joy thinks and feels. Maybe, he'll swap the point of view back later. I want to find out what happens between the two. I'll address the narration issue later.

***

My food delivery from Lewnes' arrives. Although the telluric delivery boy doesn't interest me, I give him a fair tip. I devour my juicy steak—cooked to medium-rare perfection. Lewnes' French fries are the best in the world. The peas can't match the world-famous fries.

***

While I'm confined, my productivity increases, but it would be nice to go outside. I can't complain as much as the ordinary man. My work keeps my mind off current events, and the country and world's dismal predicaments. I enjoy the view over Spa Creek. I look out in the direction of the Naval Academy's Chapel. I stare.

CHAPTER 10

THE YOUNG THAI masseuse doesn't care her American customer admitted to a drinking problem. She thinks Thai men have problems and Americans don't. Joy's village has many alcoholics. She never has seen a foreigner drunk.

"Thai man gamble. Him butterfly. Lie me. You good man. You America ka. I li-eh America man. Joy no li-eh Thai man. Him no good. Him lie me. Thai man bad. Thai man wery bad."

"I see."

"Ka."

Tom wondered if all Thai women felt the same way. American men go on and on complaining about American women, at least his Navy SEAL buddies do. American women think they're doing you a favor if you have sex; they imply you owe them in return.

"You marry?"

"No, I'm single."

"No sure. No lie Joy."

"It's true. I'm single, Joy."

"You no wife? No kid ka?"

"No wife and no kids. I'm single, Joy. Really."

"Tam mai sot?"

Joy switched into the Thai language. Tom thought she asked, "Why was he single?" He knows 'ka' is a polite word in Thai, but never knew when she would say it. He likes her throaty 'ka.'

"I never met the right woman I suppose. There is one girl, though, she really ... oh, nothing ... I'm searching for a Thai wife."

You have no idea what you're getting yourself into, Tom. A Thai woman can satisfy your sexual needs. She can do that well. Most Thai women enjoy sex as much as you, but along with her family, they'll try and soak you.

She'll be needing money to pay for a car accident her brother caused. The other brother will need a rabies vaccine, after he gets bitten by the neighbor's dog while trying to rob their house. The little sister money for school uniforms. They'll need the latest iPhone. The list will grow.

"He, he, he. Joy wery good, Doc."

"I can tell."

"Ka."

Tom marveled at how fast things moved in Bangkok. She wondered why such a rich doctor isn't married. She wondered if he's gay. Young boys from her village service gay foreigners.

"You're damn right they move fast. I'm warning you, ole boy." I find myself yelling at my screen. I blame the alcohol.

Being cooped up all day, every day, doesn't help my mental state.

"You girlfriend? Thai lady?"

"No."

"You gay, Doc? You li-eh ladyboy?"

"No, I'm not gay, Joy!"

Surprised by her customer's sensitivity, Joy remained silent. In the Navy and among Tom's SEAL brothers, everyone is macho. People never spoke about being gay or about feelings for the same sex. When those issues came up, Tom became uncomfortable.

Joy struggled to believe he is single. Either he lied, or he's gay. And, despite Tom's inexpensive clothes, the poor girl was convinced of his wealth.

Tom knows little about ladyboys. He heard that a ladyboy is a man who acts like a woman. Ladyboys can be extremely beautiful and indistinguishable from biological females—at least with their clothes on. Ladyboys are supremely skilled at sex. He remembers one sailor telling him that, "A ladyboy can suck the chrome right off a Harley's tail pipe, and I mean that literally."

When Tom's imagination started rolling, he felt uncomfortable. He closed his mouth, after an image of Bpee entered his mind. In his haste, Tom bit his lip. Joy's active hands kept her from sensing anything unusual.

Chapter 11

LADYBOY IS A THIRD gender in Thailand. According to Thai women, ladyboys are more beautiful than women. Ladyboys are much taller and have longer and firmer legs. Due to their larger frames, they get larger breast implants than Thai women.

Some ladyboys keep their male organ, while others opt for surgery. Many ladyboys are well endowed. They aren't usually shy, but rather direct and forthcoming. Their voices, Adam's apples, and large hands often give them away. But, those features too can be disguised by plastic surgeries, which typically are paid for by rich farang boyfriends.

It occurs to me that the character, Bpee, who made a pass at Tom when he first entered the massage parlor, might be a ladyboy. I feel pretty sure she is. The author is steering clear of that topic, but I'll need to look back and see if I missed any hints.

I don't want Tom getting mixed up with ladyboys. I'm prejudiced against them. I feel a bit ashamed of myself for my shortcoming. I return to the passage where Joy is questioning Tom about ladyboys.

"Doc, you prefer ladyboy?"

"I don't know much about them, Joy."

"Mai sure ka."

"I don't, Joy. I don't know about ladyboys."

"Weally?"

"Yes, Joy. Really. I'm not lying."

"Sure."

"Yes."

"Ka."

Tom didn't share the tales he'd heard about Navy men getting drunk, going home with beautiful Thai women, and then being shocked when they removed their date's underwear. Those stories rarely ended well. In some cases, angry sailors beat up ladyboys.

Tom figured such encounters happened often if he'd heard about them. Most sailors wouldn't be going around sharing such an embarrassing story. He guessed that sailors who continued after such a discovery probably never told their stories to anyone. Tom wondered how many continued.

Joy wondered if Tom was telling the truth.

"You look Bpee. Bpee look you ka."

"Bpee?"

"Bpee, taller girl in shop. Her beautiful lady ka."

"Oh, her name's Bpee. She stared at me."

He adjusted himself on the mattress.

"You look she."

"She looked at me more, Joy."

"Bpee ladyboy. You li-eh? She wery big size ka. Wery pretty. Big size mahk ka."

"Bpee's a ladyboy?"

"Ka."

"How could I be so stupid?"

Tom felt strongly attracted to Bpee. He fantasized about her. Embarrassed, he now understood how other sailors had been tricked.

"Her fool farang easy."

"She's very pretty," Tom said unintentionally. "Do you have kids, Joy?"

He asked the first question that popped into his head.

The thought of Bpee being a ladyboy never occurred to Tom. Joy's remark about her anatomy stuck in his head. He felt uncomfortable. He wondered how big she is and found himself competing. At some point, Joy had seen her naked. She called it pretty.

While thinking about Bpee, Tom became aroused. He never thought about a man before, but to him, Bpee isn't a man. She looks and behaves like a woman. He stuck with his first impression of her, but recurring images disturbed him.

"Ha, ha, ha. Joy too young for kid. Joy single. No husband ka. Joy wirgin. He, he, he."

"Really?"

Joy hesitated. While Tom gathered his thoughts, he missed her pause.

"Joy wirgin ka," she lied. Joy continued truthfully, "Mai mee fan."

"Mai mee fan?"

"No boyfriend. Joy no have boyfriend."

"Okay. I don't have a girlfriend in Thailand."

"Mai sure."

"Yes, Joy. That's true. I don't have a girlfriend here. I practically just arrived."

"Weally?"

"Yes."

"Ka."

Tom wondered about Joy's virginity. She is very young. It didn't matter to him. As the two of them chatted, she squirted more oil onto his back. She gripped the back of his neck in her hands and squeezed them firmly together. When she eased the pressure, her hands slid down, carried by gravity. The motion soothed him.

Joy repositioned herself. She spread her customer's legs and sat between them. She began rubbing him lower. First, she worked his lumbar and then the backs of his legs—from the tops of his hamstrings to the bottoms of his calves. She enjoyed the clean feel of his shaved body.

"You good skin. Joy li-eh farang skin. Thai man skin no good. Dark ka."

"Farang?"

"Farang mean for-rin-err."

"Oh, okay. Farang."

"Ka. How long you stay Thailand?"

"I just arrived."

"Weally?"

"Yes."

Tom avoided answering her directly. He isn't sure how long he needs to be in Southeast Asia. That will depend on his orders.

"You stay Bangkok?"

"Yes, for a couple of weeks. After that, I go to Chiang Mai."

"You wife Chiang Mai?"

"No, Joy! I'm single. Really, I promise. I've never been to Chiang Mai."

"Ka."

Farangs lied to Joy several times in the past, and she tried to be careful. She's interested in Tom. Their age difference never occurred to her.

"You no lie Joy. Thai man lie. Joy not li-eh lie. You no lie Joy."

"I'm not lying."

"Sure?"

"Yes, Joy."

"Chiang Mai lady beautiful. Me never go, but all Chiang Mai lady beautiful ka. People say Chiang Mai lady beautiful. All people say. Wery beautiful. Most beautiful lady in Thai. Wery good. Sexy too. He, he, he."

"Oh, okay."

"Ka."

Just as Thai women have a well-deserved reputation for lying to foreign men, in turn, they have a

well-deserved reputation for lying to Thai women.
Tom lied to Joy once already. She moved down near
his feet. She splashed oil on his hamstrings. He
wanted her to flip him.

CHAPTER 12

WHENVER JOY SPREAD oil on the Navy SEAL, he enjoyed a pleasant whiff of coconut. She used her soft hands skillfully. Unlike her toenails, she keeps her fingernails short, so she won't scratch a customer or bend back a nail. When Joy ran her fingertips over Tom's inner thighs, it tingled.

"You li-eh ka?"

"Yes, Joy. Everything you do feels good. Very good."

"Joy li-eh you ka. You strong man. Good body. Blue eye. You good man. Me chorp America man."

"You're good. I like what you're doing."

"Ka."

"Keep going."

"Ka."

"Yeah, good. Very good."

As a child, Joy had been taught that farang men are good and that she should find a farang husband to help support her family. She knows chilies are spicy, mangoes sweet, and sticky rice sticky. She knows farang men are good. Joy never learned about foreign women. She doesn't know if they are good or bad. The question never came up. She doesn't formulate many questions of her own. At school, she learned by rote.

Joy's hands moved onto Tom's buttocks. She rubbed him steadily, circling her hands. Sometimes, her hands stalled, and she pumped up-and-down vigorously a half-dozen times—each time pressing down and forward, using her entire body weight. Then, she pulled him up and backward. With each repetition, he shifted back and forth several inches on the thin mattress.

Beads of Joy's sweat dripped onto his back. She ran her fingertips over a place where no one had ever touched him. It felt good. He thought about staring at her face, once she rolled him over. Her oily hands occupied his mind. He planned to tell her to keep going.

Joy started at the tops of his hamstrings and ran her oil-covered forearms up over his cheeks to the small of his back. She leaned over and fell forward using all her strength. At the apex of her upward motion, he could feel her blowing sensuously on his shoulders. When she brought her hands back down, she again ran a set of fingers between his buttocks. With each succeeding time, he contributed to his own pleasure by shifting his body position, so her fingers touched the desired spot. She became more exploratory, as his motions granted her that permission.

The image Joy created of Bpee stuck in Tom's mind. He imagined the ladyboy behind him and raised his hips. Joy understood what he desired. He shoved his guilt aside. As he began to rock and arched his back, she did what he wanted. When he raised himself onto his toes, she reached underneath him. Joy felt something strange.

"You extra ka?"

"Yeah, I was born with three, not two."

"Weally?"

"There are only a few men in the world who have this condition."

"Weally?"

"Yes, Joy."

"Wery … wery in resting. Wery …"

"Don't worry, it's normal. Well, not normal … I'm fine. All three work fine."

"Ka … ka. He, he."

After triple checking, Joy continued. She didn't give his third testicle another thought. He wanted her to grab and squeeze him in her well-lubricated hands. The incense and dim lighting created a nice atmosphere, but the tension mounted in the room. His fantasies ran wild. He needed a release. She wanted an orgasm and a chance to get pregnant.

CHAPTER 13

TOM COULD TELL that Joy began stripping. After dragging her bra across his back, she placed it in the growing pile. Next, she dropped her skirt and panties there. Tom swallowed. Joy exhaled forcefully. She continued with a body-to-body massage.

Under the pressure, her breasts compressed against his back. She slid down the backs of his legs, traversing behind his knees, and culminating the titillating motion by blowing a puff of air between his cheeks. The stubble from her bikini wax felt like nothing he'd experienced before. Although Joy knew the answer, she asked permission to continue.

"You li-eh ka?"

"Very good, Joy. Outstanding. You're very good. Please keep going."

"Ka."

"Yeah, good."

Joy became more exploratory. He wet his lips and spread his legs farther apart. Her fingers fulfilled his fantasy. After several minutes, her imitation ended.

"Turnover. Switch to back ka."

"Okay."

"Good ka."

As he started to roll over, she assisted by pulling up on his shoulder.

"Oh! You wery, wery big. Three ball."

"Yes."

"He, he. Neung, sorng, sahm. Three ball ka."

"Yes."

"Chorp. You wery handsome man. Wery hard ka."

"Thanks."

"All ball same size."

"Yeah."

"Ka."

Joy guessed his huge size required a third ball. Nothing in her experience indicated a man might have more than two. The subject never came up. Since he had three, she realized some men did. If she saw another man this size, she figured he would have three as well.

"I like you, Joy."

"Khun lor mahk."

"You're beautiful."

"Korp khun ka."

"Sure. That's good."

"Joy want."

Tom's brain switched off, as she squirted coconut oil.

"Oil. Good ka."

"Yes. It's good."

"Dee."

"Good. Very good."

"Ka."

Joy started what he craved. He pointed his toes and stared. One oily hand began racing up and down, while the other played below. Her mouth got involved. Each time she went over the cornice, he could barely hang on. She encouraged his touch. He watched her lips.

Delaying him with a firm squeeze, Joy repositioned. She wanted his baby. He moved his hands onto her waist. When his fingers touched on opposite sides, the discovery of her true dimensions shocked him. They spoke to each other in seductive voices, but little of what they said made any sense.

Joy gyrated her hips, as she propelled herself up and down. Her eyeballs migrated up to one side. The shop girls switched their mobiles to vibrate, as they moved higher up the stairs. Bpee sat on the top step, closest to the door. Her teeth clinched. Joy's moaning added a chemical to Tom's blood stream. His rational self deserted him.

CHAPTER 14

JOY BLINKED. HIS pinching caused blood to seep from her circular areolas. The trickle merged with a salty one and flowed toward her tiny belly button. Farther downstream, the riverlets ran onto her thighs and his stomach. The colors among her breasts, areolas, and nipples created a marvelous palette. He pinched harder, employing fingernails. His frog tattoo lapped up the dripping blood.

Her body separated into pain and pleasure compartments—distinct nerve bundles that jolted her. She could no longer manage the small fires burning within. This loss of control brought her ecstasy, as she couldn't tell where the next flare-up would be. When two similar blazes merged, they produced a raging inferno—doubling her pain or pleasure. When blazes of opposite types joined, they produced a delightful calming.

Her moaning evolved into a chant. A pool of brackish water—sweat, coconut oil, blood, and internal fluids—formed in and ran out of his taut navel. Intent on hurting herself, she sprang up and down in alla breve. He thrived on her ripe energy. Summoning all the might in her trembling legs, she probed deeper inside.

Joy entered a world of good vibrations. Her face showed confusion. She clutched the sheet. With a wide-open mouth, she gulped in oxygen. Adrenaline became her fuel. One eye closed involuntarily. Her posture changed. She sprang in strong, rapid bursts. He saw tears of joy streaming down her cheeks.

"Joy coming ka …"

She shook violently and repeated the phrase over and over again. The volume increased until she was yelling. Fluids squirted every which way, as her body attempted to extinguish its raging flames. Her primitive shrills sent him back in time. The decency mankind evolved through many generations evaporated. This carnal act would finish the way the little Thai masseuse intended.

The massage girls crowded around the door. Bpee's busy hand moved quickly.

"Doc, come inside Joy! Please ka! Joy love you. Please ka …"

Bpee whispered, "Come inside me too," as she started to finish.

Tom lifted Joy up, spun her around, and positioned her facing away. He leaned back. From his praying position, he entered heaven. As with others, she couldn't see his ravaging face. She flapped helplessly, unable to fly more than a foot off the mattress. She screamed. He tugged harder. There was no stopping him.

Joy's wet hijab covered her back. Desperate, she turned and stared. Her mien pleaded mercy. She wanted him to stop; she surrendered. Her broken will trigger his victory celebration. He closed his eyes, as the fluids blasted out. When she filled up, her nails dug into his wrists.

Tom babbled. Bpee finished. Joy moaned. She clutched him. He bit his lip. The little Issarn girl wanted to get pregnant; she wanted his baby; she wanted out of the massage parlor; she wanted out of the sex industry; she wanted out of poverty. As he continued shuttering, she maintained her feisty grip. When Bpee flashed in front of his eyes, his pleasure peaked.

"Yeah, baby! Go ahead and …"

Tom realized he'd spoken out loud. He let go of a wrist and grabbed a handful of hair, half expecting it to feel like cloth. He forgot where he was.

"You okay?"

Tom hesitated. He wasn't sure. He wasn't sure why Bpee appeared, just as he orgasmed. She felt amazing though.

"Oh, yeah. You were wonderful, Joy. That was the best ever."

"You wery strong. Sexy man."

"Oh, you're wonderful. Your noises. You came so many times."

"Me come mahk, mahk ka. Dee mahk."

"Yeah, you're incredible."

"Ka."

Joy smiled. Their thrusting subsided. The mattress soaked through. He scooted back. The pop made her giggle. She turned to face him. His face was red. They embraced.

"You wery big, Doc."

"You're very small."

"Me wery small ka. You wery big ka."

"Yeah, it's a great combination."

"Ka."

"I never experienced anything like that before. Incredible."

"Ka."

Although Joy didn't know what the words meant, she agreed.

CHAPTER 15

TOM KISSED JOY on the lips for the first time. She threw her arms around him, and he held her. Joy loved kissing the handsome man. He squeezed her affectionately. She felt pleased. The lovers pressed their sweaty chests together, and they could feel their hearts pounding. Sweat dripped. She fiddled with her hair.

"Joy came ten time. No twenty. Ha, ha, ha."

"It must have been twenty."

"Ka."

"It felt so good."

She kissed and squeezed him.

"You happy?"

"Yes, I'm paralyzed with happiness. I'm more than happy! I'm delighted," he paused. "I came inside you, Joy."

Tom never came in a woman, unless he wore a condom. Due to his polyorchidism, he produces an extraordinary amount of semen. The chances of a lover getting pregnant are high. He never had unprotected sex. In Thailand, these two issues never even concerned him, until now. Their sex transpired without any responsibility. The clever little Thai girl wanted to get pregnant and married. He simply wasn't thinking. He was now.

"Thanks. You good man."

"That felt so good. I really enjoyed it."

He shook his head.

"Ka."

"Thanks, baby."

"Joy mee khwam suk."

Even in his euphoria, Tom felt troubled by the graphic image of Bpee seen at the height of his climax. He saw the ladyboy's face with great clarity. In fact, he saw more than just her face. His risqué vision brought him immense pleasure, but he felt guilty.

"Look. See?"

Tom snapped back from his troubling thoughts. The jaunty girl pointed at the bloody sheet.

"Told you. Joy wirgin. He, he, he."

"Yes, I see. Not any more, though. You're definitely not a virgin now. You're such a strong little girl. You're so lovely. That was amazing, Joy."

"Joy wery strong. Wery strong. He, he, he."

"You sure are."

"Ka."

"You're like a little Navy SEAL."

"Ka."

Joy pulled the soiled sheet off. She spread out a towel. He positioned himself on his stomach. She placed a towel over his perspiring body. After a few minutes, she put on her clothes.

"Joy came back soon. Finish massage."

"Okay."

"Me back soon."

"I'll probably fall asleep."

"Ka."

Tom marveled that she planned to finish the massage. If a girlfriend back home offered him a beer while he watched a baseball game, he got lucky. He should have been arrested for what he'd done to Joy, but instead, she planned to come back and take care of him.

He sang Young Girl—"Young girl, get out of my mind ..." The stories sailors tell about Thailand are all true. The women love to serve their men. They are great lovers. He rolled onto his side. She left him breathless with her moves. The ladyboys are drop-dead gorgeous and impossible to tell from biological females. With one final thought about Bpee, he fell asleep.

In the hallway, Joy encountered a group of scrambling masseuses. They giggled.

"You lucky girl, Joy."

"Wery lucky."

"Sanuk mai?"

"Him big size mai?"

"Sexy mai?"

"Ka, ka."

With a look of distain, ladyboy Bpee retreated down the steps last. She concealed one hand. Joy smiled on her way to shower.

Chapter 16

*S*EVERAL DAYS PASSED, *as I read and re-read my manuscript. I said 'my' manuscript because I edited the files. I made extensive changes to improve the story. I didn't save the original files, and now it's hard to remember which sections I wrote from scratch.*

Although I feel satisfied with the initial parts, I know they aren't finished. The magnitude of this task keeps me pressing forward. I'll return later. I decide to continue with JoyPart9. I make steady progress; I make edits on the fly.

The story continues in the massage room.

After Joy finished showering, she returned to a sleeping Doc. When she opened a bottle of water, he woke. Her recovery dumbfounded him.

"Me continue massage ka. Joy sorry you, Doc. You sexy man. Wery big man. Joy li-eh you wery much."

"Well, uh …"

"You angry me?"

"No. No, I'm not angry, Joy. I couldn't be angry with you."

"Me sorry you."

"It's okay. You're a very sweet girl."

"Ka. Sure?"

"Yeah."

Tom shook his head at her apology. Their rough sex, while he fantasized about Bpee, made him ashamed. He felt like he committed a crime. Joy wasn't sure how he felt. Sensing that, he provided reassurance.

"I'm happy, Joy. You're lovely and fun—an incredible lover. When you're happy, I'm happy."

"I happy."

"Then I'm happy."

"He, he, he. Ka."

"You're very good."

"Ka. You good man. America man."

Satisfied, she continued. Fatigued from intense love making, he relaxed. A trickle reminded Joy that she might get pregnant.

"You no marry?"

"Nope."

"Joy want telephone number you."

"Sure. I don't know it off the top of my head. I have a new phone. When we're done, we can exchange numbers. Okay?"

"Good."

"Sure, that'll be nice."

"Ka."

When Joy understood that she had satisfied her customer, a sense of pride welled up. She wiped him with a damp towel.

"Joy wash you. Clean ka."

"Thanks."

"Joy good girl. Me good take care."

"Yes, I see that. I feel that."

"Ka."

Joy massaged his arms and hands, and rubbed his palms vigorously. She formed a tube with her hand, and went up and down on each of his fingers. She pulled on each finger, until her hand slipped off the end. The separation made a snap.

When the massage ended, Joy wrapped Tom in a towel. This time, the other masseuses scattered before Joy opened the door. She led him to the shower.

"Here clean towel. Shower ka."

"Okay. Thanks."

"Ka."

She kissed him passionately.

"Joy wait here."

"Okay, I'll be back soon."

"Ka."

***

Tom squeezed a bunch of soap onto his hand and lathered up. He found a small brush and scrubbed off the oil. It felt much better going on than it did coming off. After rinsing with the lukewarm water, he put the shower head back.

Tom toweled off hard in an effort to wipe off any remaining oil. He felt shame. Joy brought his clothes in a basket, and he dressed in the mildewy shower room. She went to the other bathroom to finish washing up. His wallet and phone were there. He put on his watch. The session had taken over two hours.

CHAPTER 17

JOY WONDERED how her customer would react. A while later, when Doc emerged, she took his hand. They smiled. She appeared fresh. Make-up and lipstick restored her. She smelled nice. Tom marveled.

Joy led him down the narrow stairs. It seemed like an eternity since they'd come up. He'd forgotten completely about their unevenness and the florescent bulb. He'd forgotten quite a few things.

As they entered the foot-massage area, Tom could hear several masseuses chatting about them. He blushed. Only now did he realize they'd been so loud that others had heard. The sexy little Thai magician had taken him on a journey far away. He slowly returned.

"Good massage?" a fat and balding Caucasian man asked.

"Not bad."

"She's cute."

"No different than the rest. I can't recommend the service … Too young and inexperienced."

"Oh, okay. Thanks."

"Sure, anytime."

The Navy SEAL responded in an effort to avoid the unattractive man requesting a massage with Joy.

Bpee smiled at Tom. She injected more thoughts into his head. Another terribly uncomfortable image entered his mind. He wondered what it would be like to have Bpee watching him go down on her. The ladyboy seemed capable of reading his mind and touched herself provocatively. Tom rubbed his red face and looked down at his crotch. He was out of balance.

Shop girl 1 → "How massage, Mister?"

Shop girl 2 → "You li-eh?"

"Okay."

Blushing and giggling masseuse → "He, he, he."

Sexy masseuse → "Joy good girl."

"Me li-eh you."

"Thanks."

"Ka."

"You're very handsome and have an excellent shape," Bpee said.

Her voice mimicked a female's. Her English is superior to that of the other girls. Tom noticed a scar on Bpee's throat and guessed that she'd undergone vocal-cord surgery.

"Thanks a lot."

"Ka."

As Tom reclined in a foot-massage chair, Joy brought him a cup of tea. Bpee continued to stare. He sipped and stole glances at the sultry ladyboy. His imagination ran amok.

"Doc, your phone ka."

Joy held out one of her magic hands. Tom gave her the phone. He watched her tiny thumbs rapidly keying. Her phone began to play a Thai ballad. She saved his number.

"He, he, he."

"Oh, that's great. Thanks."

"Ka."

Joy returned the phone. He saved her number.

"Thanks, Joy. Good. I have your number now."

He finished the tea.

"You call me, Doc. You promise?"

Joy flashed a concerned smile. He felt sure several men had lied to her. She really wanted him to call.

"Yes, I'll call you, Joy. I promise I'll call."

"Korp khun ka."

"Sure."

Tom meant it. He would enjoy seeing Bpee again too.

"Joy love you ka," she whispered.

"Thank you so much. You're very special to me, Joy."

"Ka."

"I promise I'll call. Very soon."

"Ka."

Tom gave her hand a squeeze. When she returned the squeeze, he remembered her first touch from a few hours earlier. He grinned and stood up.

Although Tom wanted to kiss Joy good-bye, he understood that public displays of affection are against Thai culture. Given what went on behind closed doors, he wondered about the contradiction. Joy opened the slider for her American man. He pulled on his trainers, took a good look at Joy's heels among the shoes, and headed back down to Sukhumvit.

After a few moments, Tom turned. Joy stood smiling and waving. He waved back. She loved him. She believed in him. She needed him. He felt strongly for her. Bpee stood behind Joy. The ladyboy waved and blew kisses. Tom fantasized about the gorgeous ladyboy. As he turned to walk away, he heard Joy shout a warning at Bpee.

The ladyboy troubled Joy. She didn't want to lose Doc. She knows that Bpee will try and take him away. The ladyboy wanted to have sex with the handsome American. She also wanted his financial support. Bpee knew he was curious.

As Tom turned onto Soi 4 out of view, he shook his head back and forth. If the guys could see me now. All my friends told me I was crazy to come here in search of a Thai wife. They would love to have a wife like Joy. There wouldn't be any more locker-room chat about a boring sex life.

Joy found Tom. He wondered if he could marry someone so young. Bangkok inexorably changed his perspective on many things, and he'd only been there for a few days. He suddenly noticed many older men walking arm-in-arm with much younger women.

Tom is 14 years older than Joy. He'd seen guys who were in their late sixties walking around with 20-somethings. In Bangkok, couples with vast age gaps seem natural, but in the United States, people make rude and disapproving comments about such age differentials. If the couples are happy, he wondered why anyone should feel compelled to pass judgment.

As Tom continued down Soi 4, he realized that Joy hadn't even charged for his massage. He owed the shop. The next time that he saw Joy, he would make up for this oversight. He touched his wallet and smiled.

Although the Navy SEAL made an effort to keep the sexy ladyboy Bpee from entering his thoughts, he realized it was going to be hopeless. It seemed odd that he felt a loyalty to Joy already though. He never felt that way about one-night stands in the United States, but it seemed to him that his relationship with Joy was going to be more than that, and possibly much more.

Graphic images of Bpee kept appearing to Tom. They were enjoyable images that made him feel excited, but he wasn't comfortable enough with his own sexuality to accept them. In the military, he learned a "don't ask, don't tell" rule, but for those who are attracted to the same sex, there is a deep guilt and shame associated with such feelings.

At first sight, Bpee was one of the most beautiful and sexy women whom Tom had ever seen. No transsexual had ever hit on him before, at least not that he noticed. Prior to meeting Bpee, he never thought about being with such a woman. To him, she is more female than male. She looks, sounds, and acts female. Most people who met her would think she is a woman. He concluded Bpee is female. Once convinced, he cleared the path for any future encounters with the pretty ladyboy.

Tom wondered if Joy was truly in love with him. He believes in love at first sight. He possessed strong feelings for Joy, but wondered if it was just desire and lust. She is so free, simple, and sexy. Her voice so sweet and innocent. Similarly to him, she seems to have an insatiable appetite for sex.

Tom is in Thailand now, and he doesn't want to think too much. Bangkok won't allow him to think too much. He loved being with Joy. He planned to keep meeting with her. If his feelings grow, maybe he'll pop the big question.

Bargirls, the traffic jam, hawkers, men offering women, and the crowd on the sidewalk captured little of the Navy SEAL's attention. He needed to accomplish what he'd come to Thailand to do. He adjusted his shorts. With a huge grin on his face, he walked on in search of a bar and a strong drink.

CHAPTER 18

ALTHOUGH IT SEEMS impossible, I grew tired of the mouth-watering steaks and sides from the award-winning Ruth Chris's Steakhouse and Lewnes' Steak House. I now rotate my take-out orders among Lemon Grass, Carlson's Donuts and Thai Kitchen, and Nano Asian Dining. The only one with a Thai-sounding name is Lemon Grass. Although pricey and serving Americanized-Thai food, the meals from Lemon Grass are passable. Carlson's serves delicious and authentic Thai food, and their do-nuts are amazing. The odd combination delivers me a Thai dinner and an American breakfast.

Nano isn't Thai food at all, but more what in America, we call Asian fusion. I usually order their sashimi and sushi. The sushi rolls are filling. The ample wasabi produces the head-clearing nasal burn that one needs while eating raw fish. They give you plenty of raw ginger. I hope one of my delivery girls will look like Joy, and offer her services, but so far, no one tempts me. And, no one has offered her services. My total immersion in this project has me thinking unusual thoughts.

I'm in a routine. After splashing my face with ice water and taking a few Ibuprofens, I eat two chocolate-frosted Carlson's donuts and drink a cup of ginger tea. I make ice to replace what has been lost the previous evening. I stare out the window at the Naval Academy's Chapel. I sit down at my dining-room table, and I start work on the novels.

By mid-afternoon, I'm drinking Maker's Mark. In the evening, I pause for my delivered dinner. Since I'm not going out of the Tecumseh on most days, I find myself pacing around the apartment. I often plan to take work into the bedroom, but I usually pass out somewhere between the refrigerator and the printer.

Tom and Joy are getting along well.

On a mid-November evening, Tom texted Joy that he wanted to come see her the next day for a two-hour massage. She delighted in getting his message, and she replied immediately. With that meeting confirmed, he looked forward to his appointment. She could hardly wait to see her handsome, frog-tattooed customer again.

Having been in Thailand for a couple of weeks, Tom was getting over his jetlag. However, Bangkok's heat and his alcohol consumption kept him in a state of fatigue. Still, he felt himself getting stronger day by day.

When Tom walked out onto Sukhumvit Road these days, he knew exactly where he was going. While passing through the area around Nana Plaza Soi 4, things seemed much calmer and even organized. The street's activities didn't overwhelm his senses. He recognized many landmarks and even people from the preceding days. The city forced its inhabitants to follow a daily routine.

"Massage, Mister? Handsome man. Welcome ka."

Tom kept walking. He no longer turns his head for such invitations.

"Where you go? Tuk-tuk, sir?"

He ignored the scrawny man.

Taxi driver → "Taxi, taxi."

Scruffy roadside man → "Need sexy girl, Boss?"

"Tuk-tuk? Taxi?"

"Me have many good girl. Cheap."

A squirrelly Thai man shoved a laminated sheet in front of the Navy SEAL's face. The worn, plastic advertisement depicted dozens of photos of numbered, beautiful, and scantily clad Thai women. The American ignored the pimp and kept walking.

Tom's body ached from a lack of any real exercise. He hadn't resumed his normal workouts. He was accustomed to lifting heavy weights three times per week. On many days, he cross-trained doing martial arts, cycling, or swimming. He often walked around carrying a heavy backpack too.

The relaxed state induced by the Navy SEAL's physical exertion contributed to him sleeping more soundly, and releasing aggressive tendencies. They're caused by his three testicles, producing a far-greater amount of testosterone than normal. His recent physical activity came from sessions with Joy, and short walks in steamy Bangkok.

When he arrived at Lucky Massage, a happy and smiling Joy greeted him. He removed his sandals, and she placed them in the shoe pile next to her heels. She squeezed his hand and led him in.

The massage girls became used to seeing the muscular American and hardly looked up from their mobiles. They realized he isn't interested in them. Although Tom searched, he didn't find Bpee. Joy hurried her man past the foot-massage room, and they went to their private room. She dead bolted the door and began helping her lover undress.

They enjoyed fantastic sex, and she gave him a relaxing massage afterwards. With each successive meeting, the young Issarn girl's fear that she wouldn't hear from or see her ideal man again diminished. She gained confidence. Tom wanted to see her every day. They were both happy.

After Tom showered, he paid Joy 2,000 baht. Although the two-hour massage cost only 600, he tipped her 1,400. It helped to support her family. It seemed like ages ago, since his first visit, when he forgot to pay. He learned she had paid the 600 baht. When he had returned, he made that up to her. Her arithmetic skills are weak.

Each time Tom left, Joy felt sad. Her mood rubbed off on him. When he reached the Indian tailor's shop, he turned back to see her waving. He smiled, waved, and continued walking. Already, just a couple weeks into their relationship, the lovers fell into patterns. In his line of work, it's dangerous to form habits. As an uneducated girl, she doesn't think about patterns. Their relationship blossomed, and she fell deeply in love.

Whenever Tom encountered Bpee, she acted friendly. He enjoyed chatting with her and seeing her beautiful body. Although he fantasizes about sex with Bpee, he loves Joy. He believed their relationship is going somewhere special.

Joy became uncomfortable with the situation at Lucky Massage, and asked if she could come to Tom's room rather than have him visit the shop. He obliged. They started spending more time together, as she hoped, and often stayed the night. He continued to think about Bpee during sex. He missed seeing her.

Although Joy never asked Tom for any money, when she visited, he always gave her 2,000 baht. With each succeeding visit, she took the payment more for granted. He knew she had to pay the shop 500 baht for an outcall. She used a tuk-tuk to go to and from his hotel. Even after expenses, she earned good money.

Tom had trained Joy to expect a generous payment. He felt happy to pay her initially, but now, he had no choice. If he stopped paying, she would assume something was terribly wrong. The poor girl depended on his financial support.

Joy's wardrobe improved with Tom's payments, and she acquired several items that she always had dreamed of owning. With her steady income, many shops extended her credit. She bought a cover for her phone, earrings, a corset, bras and panties, a skirt, cosmetics, jeans, a ring, a charm bracelet, and a watch.

Joy expanded her collection of stilettos too. The heels make her feel sexy and confident. She loves wearing them for him. She likes to feel tall. On a regular basis, Joy sent money back home. She too had trained them to expect regular payments.

Both Joy and her family's standard of living increased significantly because of the money from her boyfriend. Over a short time, her family members adjusted to an improved life style, which they all expect to continue. She needs to keep pleasing her primary lover.

CHAPTER 19

ALTHOUGH I FEEL happy for Tom and his sex life with his Surin girlfriend, I worry about him. He will get bored with the lovely little Thai girl. A man with his record-setting testosterone level won't get bored of sex, but the poor Issarn girl's lack of education will come to trouble him. She isn't old enough to have finished tenth grade.

From my knowledge and what the author tells us, Joy probably dropped out of sixth grade. Along with the narrator's material, I blend in a few paragraphs relating to Joy. As an authority on bargirls and a Nobel laureate, the original author won't mind. If anything, he'll thank me.

Although brilliant at reading a man's desires, Joy could barely read and write in Thai. She couldn't read English. If Tom ever becomes fluent in Thai, he'll find out that her knowledge-base is miniscule. She doesn't have any critical-thinking skills because she learned by rote. In her village, most people believe young girls don't need an education. A girl needs a rich husband. Young Joy was never encouraged to learn and never took an interest in school.

Joy knows a few national songs and the custom of coming to attention at 8 AM and 6 PM every day for the Thai national anthem. The song holds little meaning for her though, and on most days, she doesn't interrupt her routine for it. She knows farmers have dark skin. She knows wealthy Thai men prefer light skin. Although she can't write either name, she knows the names of the two most famous Thai kings: Chulalongkorn and Bhumibol.

But, like the majority of Thai women, particularly Issarn farm girls, poor little Joy knows almost nothing of history, politics, science, mathematics, medicine, the arts, economics, or geography. You can stick a Thai in front of any of these subjects too. She knows nothing of Thai history, Thai politics, Thai geography, and so on.

Joy knows that a piece of candy costs one baht. She knows the prices for noodles, kow dtom, som tam, and moo dat deo. She can't tell you what they are though. After a purchase, she can't count her change. Although she doesn't understand what the number combinations mean, she knows 7-11 is open 24-7. She knows her family always needs more money, and that gold is good—pretty and expensive.

And, Joy knows how to give a great happy ending, which a cheap customer will pay 500 baht for and a good customer, 1,000. Although she knows 1,000 is more than 500, she doesn't know that it's twice as much. She doesn't understand fractions or percentages. Whatever a calculator says, she believes.

Joy's hands learned their trade by instruction from other shop girls, observation, and friendly customers. Her complete lack of knowledge about physiology often trips her up on customers over 50, those who have been drinking, and men who are double dipping.

I'm not going to worry too much about you, Tom. I just wish the Thai government did more to educate the nice people from Issarn, people such as Joy. Maybe things will last with her, and maybe they won't. You've been through a lot, and I'm sure that you'll get through this okay.

After saving my additions, I move into the file Joy-Part15. I need to keep going ... there is much to do.

Late in the morning one day, Tom's phone vibrated. He received a message from Joy. He smiled. It always challenges him to figure out what the illiterate girl's texts mean.

"Lov u dr joy came see u night at 7ka. Joop, joop ka."

When Tom saw she had given him two kisses, he grinned. He texted her a quick reply, making sure to include two kisses.

"Thanks, baby. See you tonight at 7 PM. You're so sexy! Joop, joop."

Tom put his public phone away. He knows that Joy can't read English, so he keeps his responses short. When she arrives, he hopes she'll be wearing her new red stilettos with the black straps. The heels show off her lovely toes and legs. He dreams about what they'll do together.

Joy often brings Thai food for dinner. She comes with either khao ka moo, gai yaang khao neaw, kway teaw ladna, or tom yum goong for the main course, and khao neaw ma muang or som-o for dessert. She always arrives with two cups of cha nom yen. Tom enjoys learning about and eating Thai dishes. Gradually, he began to eat spicier food.

Joy takes good care of her boyfriend, and he happily eats whatever food she brings. In the United States, girlfriends never provided him such good care. He is the center of her universe. He loves her attention. She makes every effort to try and please him.

Before Joy departs, Tom always gives her an extra few-hundred baht. This amount easily covers the cost of their food and drinks. She expects and relies on this money; she pockets at least 100 baht for herself. Because no one in Joy's village trusts banks, she keeps cash.

I figure Tom must miss Lewnes' Steakhouse. Gai yaang khao neaw tastes good, but grilled chicken with sticky rice can't compare to a giant porterhouse steak with delicious sides. I miss Thai food, but probably not as much as Tom is missing the food here in Annapolis—the blue crabs. I substitute Maker's Mark for Tom's Thai ice tea. I continue.

Now that Joy considers the handsome American her steady boyfriend, there isn't much for her to do when she is alone. In Bangkok, the Surin girl only knows the girls at Lucky Massage. She has no friends in the city. When she isn't staying with him, she sleeps at the massage parlor with the other girls, including ladyboy Bpee. Joy lets the masseuses at the shop skip over her in the massage queue, and this gesture wins her favor.

For the moment, Joy has plenty of money. She doesn't want to massage anyone, except her handsome American boyfriend. She took herself off the market. Joy doesn't want to please any other customers. Everyone who chooses her wants a happy ending. The girls made fun of Joy and teased her about being in love. She loves her rich American man and only hopes that he loves her back.

Tom checked his watch, and it was already past noon. He wondered if Joy was having lunch with the girls at Lucky Massage. She told him they all purchased street food, usually som tam, and ate together every day.

Tom wondered if Bpee spoke to Joy about him. He felt certain she did. He hopes Bpee didn't bother Joy too much. He worries Bpee might try to interfere with their relationship. She shows great interest in the American.

The Navy SEAL glanced at his watch again. This time he noticed it's November 20th. The home office would be contacting him soon. He began thinking about the events that led him to Thailand. It all started half-way around the world back at Fort Meade, Maryland, a few months earlier …

CHAPTER 20

I'M STARING AT THE Naval Academy's Chapel, when my phone rings.

"Hi, Mom."

"Hi, darling. I'm so glad I caught you."

"I'm staying in, Mom. Call anytime. I've been meaning to call you and Dad."

"Well, that's actually why I'm calling. Your father's ill. He caught corona."

"Oh, dammit. Sorry to hear that, Mom. Terrible news. Where is he?"

"They took him to Providence Medical Center."

"Where are you?"

"I'm home. He insisted he go alone. The hospital staff wouldn't allow me to go. He had a cough for a few days. Then he got a fever. You know your father. He didn't want to go. But, when he lost his sense of taste and smell, and his fever didn't subside, I thought he must have it. He coughed. Anyway, we knew it was serious."

"What about you? How do you feel?"

"I feel fine. We've been careful. Wiping surfaces, washing hands while singing happy birthday, and wearing masks, once we suspected your father."

"Yeah, but you were exposed. Get tested."

"Things are a mess with testing. It's hard to get a test done. Unless you're sick, they don't test. I don't want to go out. I'm fine. Don't worry, darling."

"Oh, Mom. Be careful. If you feel sick at all, get to the hospital. When you can, please get tested. How's Dad taking it?"

"He seems okay. He's planning a full recovery. You know him. He's a tough old goat."

"Well, keep me posted. Do you have his number? I'll call him."

Mom gives me the telephone and room numbers. She explains how she is missing her walks and feels cooped up. I tell her I'm working on a book series. I spare the details. She tells me her food deliveries usually contain an extra item, or something is missing. I don't bother to share my setup.

I let her know my starting date at the Naval Academy is delayed. Although I detect some disappointment, she understands things are a bit crazy, even at the Academy. We talk about my professorship, and I tell her how supportive the Dean is. I discuss plans for the Midshipmen, and she gives me her thoughts. We end on a positive note. I ask her to keep me posted.

I call the Providence Medical Center, and a polite Asian-sounding woman connects me.

"Hello. Dad?"

"Hi, it's good to hear … your voice, son," my father says between coughs.

"I just got off the phone with Mom. How are you?"

"To be honest, not good … a high fever and a nasty … cough. Remember how you … sounded when you … got back from Bhutan? Well, I'm coughing … coughing worse."

"Sorry to hear that. Mom is worried, and frankly, so am I."

"Well, they have good staff. Many are Brown … or Harvard educated. Not too much you can … do. I do … what … what they tell me. I'll get through … it. Don't worry."

"Follow nurses and doctors' orders. Okay?"

"I will. Hey, there … was a guy … in the bed next to me who just … died—an Italian guy from Cranston. Real-nice … real-nice fellow—Vinnie. He caught it in North Providence … and was here for … a few days. He was coughing … like hell. Spitting up … blood.

"No matter what they … did, his cough never got … better. Vinnie wanted … spaghetti and meatballs … every day. You should have seen that … guy eat. He could … really … really eat. Like you, when … you were a teenager. Real-nice guy. I'm starting … to sound as bad … as bad as Vinnie."

"You're probably stronger than he was, Dad."

"Don't think so. He was … a young … guy. His family couldn't get … get in to see … him. I think he left … a wife and two … three kids. He worked at … the A-C-I. It's … terrible."

"Um, sorry, Dad … Well, hang in there."

"Your mother … has a copy of … our wills and …"

"Aww, don't talk like that. I'm sure you'll pull through. Mom needs you. I need you. We all need you."

"They don't … understand … this disease. The doctors are … running … running around scared. The medical staff are uptight … and overworked. I … think a few staff … got sick and … died. From the inside, you get a different … perspective, and see … how bad things … are.

"I caught this at … Rotary. Make sure you take … necessary precautions. Social distancing, mask wearing … avoid going out, to the … the extent possible. Get your food … delivered from a reputable source."

"I will, Dad. I'll talk to the staff. Make sure they're doing everything they can. I'll be in touch, and call Mom regularly."

"Thanks. You know we're … both extremely … proud of you. You've done … great things. And, we're delighted you … that professor … ship at the Academy. Go … Navy! It's one of the … greatest institutions in the … in the world. You know Jimmy

Carter went there. And, you're doing … a wonderful thing for our … for our country."

"Thanks, Dad. You know it means most, when I hear it from you."

I decide not to fill him in on the details of my leave. If Mom wants, she can tell him. Or, we can wait until he recovers. There isn't any point in adding stress.

"Hey, my nurse just … came in … came …"

Dad continues coughing.

"Listen … she says I need … to get … off the phone. The talking seems to be … irritating my … cough."

"Okay, Dad. Take care. I'll be in touch. Love you."

"Good-bye. Love … you too …"

I hear a final cough.

Mom had said the hospital staff took my Dad's mobile away. I don't mind calling him through the switchboard. Poor Vinnie—hearing the young Italian succumbed depresses me.

I stare out at the Naval Academy's Chapel. I'm deeply concerned about my father. The tragedy is we can't visit. Other than hospital staff, he is alone, in a sterile environment. He's a tough man. I don't want him to die without any family there. He probably isn't going to die.

I need to stay positive. Although my Dad is sick, I try and get my mind off his condition. I turn my concern into energy, and I return to *The Thai Wife Series of Novels* ...

CHAPTER 21

DR. CODY JONES is an expert in cryptography and the Division Director of the Intelligence-Gathering Group at the National Security Agency (NSA). He no longer engages in software and hardware development, but manages and makes decisions. He's Tom's boss at the agency. Jones is an intelligent, patriotic, and fair man.

Tom worked with him for a number of years at Fort Meade, Maryland at the NSA. They made important breakthroughs. Their work resulted in saving many American lives. Since their work is top secret, few people know about their accomplishments. They don't work for personal recognition, but rather out of service for their country.

Dr. Jones believes Tom's reputed history of violence during missions and his obsessive-compulsive behavior isn't a threat to national security, but at the agency, other politically motivated individuals don't agree. Despite Tom's extraordinary computing skills and specialty training, some feel he is too much of a risk.

Others think the Navy SEAL has a serious drinking problem. Dr. Jones views Tom as a unique asset. But, as the evidence mounted, especially in the area of Tom's mistreatment and abuse of female extremists, Dr. Jones was forced to fire him.

On September 11th, almost two months prior to Tom's arrival in Thailand, Dr. Jones called Tom in to a private meeting at the agency. Tom suspected something serious. Rather than meeting in a less-conspicuous place, Jones believed conducting the meeting in his office would raise fewer suspicions.

I didn't realize Tom was in such hot water. The narrator begins retelling the story of Tom's firing.

"Sit down, Tom."

"Thank you, sir."

"This isn't easy for me."

"Appreciate that, sir."

Tom knows that Dr. Jones is on his side—a close friend and also one of his father's.

"You're a remarkable man, Tom. One of the most valuable assets at Tenth Fleet and the NSA. Number one in your Academy's class—the Medal of Honor, two Navy Crosses, and a Silver Star. You're a real hero.

"But beyond that, you've been a pioneer in the development of our offensive and defensive cyber operations, incorporating your battlefield experience. Your work in information warfare has reshaped the Navy's thinking. The exploits you developed and deployed, in Stuxnet-derivative worms targeting SCADA systems, have saved many lives. You've made great contributions.

"Your cyber, sniping, and SEAL-specialty skills are a unique combination. Impeccable, Tom. But, you've rubbed a few key people the wrong way. I read the reports and heard things got out of control.

"The psychoanalyst labeled you as an obsessive-compulsive sex addict. She attributed it to your exceptionally high testosterone level. You don't have to tell me what you did behind enemy lines. This is a political machine, Tom. People are concerned about your drinking too. I warned you. There's nothing I can do."

Tom regretted letting down his mentor and close friend.

"It's okay. I understand ... I've been in situations, where ... I just try to watch ... watch my brothers' backs, and I know they've got mine. My goal has always been to ... to complete missions successfully. Do I have regrets? Sure, I did some things ... things I'm not proud of ...

"People who aren't there, civilians, they can't understand ... this shit ... warfare ... deceit ... urges. The rage and hatred builds when you see a brother blown to bits. We are soldiers ... we're also humans. I don't need to tell you ... But, I've always wanted to serve my country. Serve it well ... serve it with honor. You know that."

"I'm on your side."

"Sorry, I let you down, sir. When they brought me back from Iraq the last time ... I didn't know if I could survive ... sitting behind a computer. My thoughts ... A few times I probably crossed the line with my drink and actions. There are some images ... you can't erase. Things you do in the heat of the moment. You're not rational in war. You're not sure where the line is ... it depends on the person drawing it."

"Believe me, I understand things get complicated, even if others don't. Although I want to help, there's nothing I can do. My hands are tied. You've angered senior staff. Upset people. There's the incident with that female reporter. We don't need the media involved again in any way, shape, or form. They've done enough damage.

"The pressure's been mounting from the top ... I have to let you go. I have my orders, Tom ... I'm extremely sorry."

"I know rules are rules, Cody. That was the first thing I learned at the Academy. They instilled that in us. I did mess up ... I ... I made some mistakes ... some bad ones ... We've been through a lot. I would ... do anything for my country. I'm a patriot. My father attended the Academy. He gave his life ... in the line of service ... I'd do the same."

"How can I ... put this? There's no ... good way. Officially, Tom, you're done. You no longer work for the United States government. Your career here is over ... I'm sorry to say it ... it gives me great pain. I know it comes as a tremendous blow to your father's memory.

"You wanted to make your family proud. You've done that ... had some wonderful successes. Those have been acknowledged. No one can take them away. You've saved lives ... created a new branch of cyber operations."

With hands on his knees, Tom sat listening. He could only nod at Dr. Jones. Everything was true.

CHAPTER 22

D R. JONES HANDED Tom some papers written on in pencil. Cody raised an index finger to his lips. Tom began reading.

Hand this note back to me after you've read it. I'll destroy it. I have a plan for you in the Asia-Pacific region. You're going to work undercover out of Thailand. You'll be based in the northern city of Chiang Mai. The change of scenery will do you good. Blend in as a tourist and play the local scene. Avoid the law. All your contact will be through a former Navy SEAL who resides in Bangkok. His name is Ryan Daniels. No one knows anything about this plan except for me, Ryan, and one high-ranking official.

Ryan is funded off a special budget. He'll take care of you. I'll work things out here. Memorize Ryan's number, 089 004 6693. After you've been in Bangkok for two weeks, arrange a meeting with him. Ryan has contacts all over. He's a clever guy, top-secret clearance, and dependable.

If anything happens to you, I have to deny any of this took place. You're acting alone. This note soon won't exist.

After a few weeks in Bangkok, go to Chiang Mai and settle down. You'll be there under the pretext of finding a Thai wife. Daniels will provide you with instructions and get you work. It'll be slow at first. Be patient. We're working through some issues.

With all the persistent threats and the possibility of a full-scale cyberwar, the country needs you. The Chinese, Russians, Iranians, and North Koreans are real cyber threats. We know others are working to develop their capabilities.

Nation states are meddling in our elections and manipulating our stock markets. The last market crash was caused by Chinese exploiting a backdoor in server hardware the exchange bought from them. You understand these threats as well as anyone. We need them to stop.

There is a high-level female Chinese agent operating in Thailand. Daniels hasn't been able to identify her. We believe she's working for the PLA and is a serious threat. She is described as extremely attractive, white-porcelain skin, and tall. I wish I had more. Her identity needs to be uncovered.

Daniels thinks she's onto him. She needs to be eliminated. We can't take any chances.

You and I will have limited direct contact. We simply can't be linked. The consequences for everyone involved and the ramifications are too great. I wish things could have turned out differently, but you're getting a second shot.

Important work awaits you, and I wish you all the best. Make your father and the country proud. He was a good friend. I'm going to miss you here, but you can do positive things there.

In time, maybe we'll be able to bring you back. After the dust settles, I hope to inform the top brass and sway their opinions. That's our goal. Stay out of trouble and stay safe. Good luck, son. Make our country proud!

When Tom finished reading, he felt a sense of redemption. Although his official career was finished, he would continue working undercover. The behavior that got him dismissed was being viewed as useful. Being off the radar, he wouldn't have to play strictly by the rules.

Dr. Jones had observed Tom carefully—to assure himself that Tom understood the conditions in his note. Tom committed fully to the assignment. Based on his evaluation of Tom, Cody decided to go forward, exactly as he and his superior had discussed.

Tom memorized Daniels's number, 0-8-9-0-0-4-6-6-9-3. He handed the paper back. Jones folded the note and put it into his pocket. The two cyber-security experts smiled at each other, and only because of the seriousness of the situation, were they able to restrain their laughter in the use of such a primitive communication mechanism.

They know that inside the NSA, it's critical not to leave any digital footprint. Any electronic media is easily traceable, but when Cody burned this note, their communication would be completely unrecoverable. They defeated Locard's Principle by going old school.

"Tom, I'm counting on you. America's counting on you."

"Thanks, Cody. Thanks for believing in me. At a young age, my father instilled in me a desire to serve this great nation. Four years a Midshipman in Annapolis reinforced that. SEAL training in California and Virginia ... dirty missions ... loss of life, battling the enemy, my work at NSA ... the dangerous threats to our way of life, all that, and now this ... this has only increased my desire to serve. I'll serve with honor ... I ... I will not disappoint you, sir."

"I know you'll do whatever we need, Tom. You're one of the best this nation's ever produced. If I had my way, you wouldn't be leaving at all. You're going freelance, as a secret asset. Watch your back, Tom. Don't trust anyone, except Daniels. Good luck. I'll miss you around here."

"Good-bye, Dr. Jones ... Cody, and thanks, sir. I promise you ... you won't regret this."

"I know I won't. Good-bye, Tom. It's been an honor and privilege."

"Likewise, sir."

The two men saluted each other; they embraced. They wondered if they would ever see each other again.

Chapter 23

MISS CAM-TU NGUYEN emailed a few days earlier asking where I would like the package from the Dean's Office delivered. After several exchanges, we agreed neither one of us could possibly have the coronavirus. I hardly left my apartment for the past couple of weeks, and she worked from home. When she goes to work, they check her temperature. She never had a fever. Cam-Tu will stop by. I stare out the window at the Naval Academy's Chapel.

Right on schedule, the downstairs bell rings, and I buzz in Miss Nguyen. I shaved this morning and check my look in the mirror. I fiddle with my hair and shirt. She knocks politely; I open the door.

"Hi, please come in."

"Thank you. I have package. Here you guy. I sorry; I mean go."

Miss Nguyen seems comfortable, despite her Freudian slip. I close the door. Cam-Tu looks more beautiful than I remember. She takes great care of her appearance. My lack of contact makes me more social.

"Would you care to sit down?"

"Okay."

My notes about *The Thai Wife Series of Novels*, laptop, Thai/English dictionary, note pad, and printouts cover the table, so we sit down on the sofa.

"It's nice to see you again."

"You too."

"May I call you Cam-Tu?"

"CT fine."

"Okay. Thanks, CT. You can call me Doc."

I steal Tom's nickname.

"Doc?"

"Yes."

"Okay."

"How are things at the office? Are there any Midshipmen around?"

"Him Dean working home, like me. No one Nimitz most day. I went get package and no see anyone hardly. The Yard no one; it empty."

"This coronavirus thing is scary. My Dad is sick in the hospital."

"Oh, I sorry hear that. I guess you can't see."

"No, I can't visit him. We talk on the phone. My Mom and I are worried. She's worried sick. He has a terrible cough. It's hard to get reliable information. He's in Rhode Island. I know they're doing their best. He doesn't seem to be getting stronger.

"The guy in the bed next to him died—a young Italian guy. His name was Vinnie. My Dad said the guy ate spaghetti all the time. The hospital staff aren't really sure what medicine to give Dad. He hasn't been responding well to what they've tried. Too much misinformation and uncertainty. People are losing their minds. People are dying."

"I sorry. Very crazy. I hope Dad you recover soon."

"Thanks. Me too. Do you know anyone who has the virus?"

"I think couple student get it. I don't know anyone. I alone here. I don't have family Maryland."

"You live alone?"

"Yes. Just working."

I don't want to get too personal and scare her away. So, I let her do the talking.

"I help Dean prepare material you. You go sa … sabbat …"

"Sabbatical."

"You leave one year?"

"It's a leave, but I'm planning to be working here, in Annapolis. I don't actually leave and go somewhere … I'm not going anywhere."

"Oh, that good."

"I'm working on a writing project. No one knows much about it. It's not a big secret or anything, but being cooped up in the room all day, well, there's really been no one to talk. I haven't seen anyone, except my food-delivery people.

"Do you have plans for dinner tonight? I would like it if you could stay. I have food delivered here. Today, I'm getting Thai food from Lemon Grass. Do you like Thai food? I always order more than I can eat alone."

"That kind you. I probably … I like Thai food."

"I have plenty arriving, and I could use the company."

I imagine that Miss Nguyen feels lonely too. She can use a friend, maybe even more. These are strange times. She's thinking. I cross my fingers.

"Okay. I stay."

"Oh, that's great, CT. The food usually gets here around six. Can I fix you a drink?"

"Okay."

"Any requests?"

"Oh, no. I have whatever you have."

"I drink Maker's Mark. I can fix you that with 7Up."

"Okay. Sure. What Mark Make?"

"You'll see. It's very good."

"Okay. You say so."

Cam-Tu's body is tiny. I decide to give her mostly 7Up. Although Thai women are heavy drinkers, I don't know about Vietnamese women. I add little Maker's Mark to her glass. I reverse the proportions for me.

"Here you go, CT."

"Thank you."

"Cheers."

"Cheer."

We click glasses. We sit close to each other on the couch. She seems comfortable. Our conversation flows.

"How long have you been working for the Dean?"

"Well ... academy two year."

"Have there been many cases of the coronavirus in Vietnam?"

"No. Almost none. No one die."

"Oh, that's good. Very good. We have a much bigger problem here. Europe's been suffering."

"Many case here. Many case. Many die. Too many die ... America people no like mask. Asia people wear mask. We wear mask pollution. We no mind mask. Mask normal Asia people."

"Is that drink okay?"

"Sweet, not strong. Good taste."

"Just let me know if you prefer something else."

"It good."

"Maker's Mark is made in Kentucky—a southern state. It's bourbon. The only place in the world that makes bourbon is Kentucky. If it isn't from Kentucky, it isn't bourbon."

"Oh ... I not drink often. Never try Mark Make before."

I wanted to tell CT I don't drink often, but I couldn't.

"I'm glad you like it."

"You nice apartment. Good view."

"Oh, here. Let me show you around. Sorry."

I take CT's hand. She smiles and holds mine. I lead her around.

"Here's the bathroom. Just help yourself."

I feel silly having said that.

"Oh, it big. My place small. Many mirror."

"My bedroom. Closet. Dresser for clothes."

"You apartment big."

"Well, you saw the living room already. There's a second bedroom … a pantry."

"A pan … pan tree?"

"Yes," I say while opening the door. "The pantry is for storing kitchen supplies and food."

"Oh. Vietnam no pan tree. Kitchen small. You much food. Vietnam no store food. Shop every day."

"Stove, oven, microwave, tea pot."

"You drink tea? Most America not like tea."

"I like ginger tea."

I lead Cam-Tu the other way.

"What do you think of my view?"

"Oh, there," CT says pointing. "I see Naval Academy Chapel. And, many boat park. I like view chapel. Good view."

"Thanks. Me too. I sometimes find myself staring out at the chapel. I …"

The doorbell rings and the food arrives. This time a cute Thai girl makes the delivery.

"Thanks. Thanks very much. Here you go," I say while handing the girl an unusually large tip. "Hope to see you again soon."

"Thanks, Mister. Bim work at The King and I. Substitute only one day here. You order King and I next time ka."

"Okay, I will."

"You li-eh."

"Yes."

"See you ka."

"Bye."

The mischievous Thai delivery girl smiles beautifully. I'm glad that Miss Nguyen hasn't gone to the door with me. I plan to order from The King and I soon. I bring in the food.

"Do you mind eating from the sofa? I have my work spread out on the dining-room table. If it's okay with you? I'm informal."

"Oh, fine. Sure. Fine."

"Oh, great. Let's see what we have. I forgot to ask you if you like spicy food."

"Spicy fine."

"I figured you did. Okay. Here we have coconut soup with chicken, spring rolls ... fried rice with shrimp, plain white rice ... noodles ... yellow mango with sticky rice for dessert. The soup and this sauce are spicy. I take out some of the prick-kee-noo chilies. They're the little green ones."

"I fine."

"Okay."

I get plates and bowls. CT assists.

"That lot food."

"Do you use chopsticks?"

I can't take that question back.

"Yes, those fine."

"Of course, oops. Please dig in and enjoy."

"Dig in?"

"I'm sorry. Americans use idioms. Short phrases. 'Dig in' means go ahead and eat. We say 'dig in' to mean start eating."

"Thank."

"English is such a hard language to learn."

CT nods in agreement. She blushes.

"Vietnamese hard too."

"Yes, I bet it is. I speak some Thai."

"Good."

CHAPTER 24

CAM-TU AND I ARE halfway through our meal and getting along well. We compare our grips for chopsticks. She uses them at home. I learned to use them in Thailand. I'm attracted to her, and she seems to feel good about me. I'm not sure where things are heading. I don't want to move too quickly.

When my phone rings, I'm in the process of fixing us another drink. I see it's my Mom calling, so I pick up.

"Hello, Mom."

"Your father's dead."

I fall down.

"Oh, noooooo."

I hear my mother crying.

"Your father's dead," my Mom repeats.

"Oh, Mom."

"We were talking. Your Dad told me he loves me, and how proud he is of you. Then, he went into a coughing fit. I heard him say, 'You've ... you've fulfilled me. I love you, darling.' I said, 'I love you too, sweetheart, forever.' He kept coughing and hacking. I may have screamed 'Help.' I didn't hear him cough. I heard the phone drop. It was terrible … terrible … I heard a nurse call out 'Doctor, doctor.'

"While the medical staff tried to revive him, I listened. I don't think they realized your father's phone was connected … I couldn't bear it. The doctor and nurse … they did all they could. We lost your Dad quickly … I don't think … I hope he wasn't in too much pain. They sounded distraught and yelled.

"I stopped listening … I didn't want to hang up. That meant losing the final connection. I longed to hear his voice one more time. I left my phone on, but I didn't listen. Not really anyway. I guess … I guess … I sort of did. I'm not really too sure … now. I put my phone down … I … I … I wanted to pick it up again, but I didn't … It died."

"Oh, Mom. That must have been so … so difficult. I wish I could have been with Dad or you … I wish we could have been together."

I cry loudly and CT comes to my side. She puts an arm around me and rubs the back of my neck.

"You were with me … and your father. I … I better go …"

I hear my mother crying; she hears me crying. Our pain is unbearable.

"Mom … Mom … okay, Mom. We can …"

"I'll call you. Love you."

"Love you, Mom."

She hangs up. I do too. I wipe my eyes. CT squeezes me. My head spins. I feel a hole in my heart. It's been shredded. I hurt. My father died alone in a hospital. The only consolation is my parents were on the phone.

I can't shake the thought of my father being alone. He coughed himself to death. My Dad must have struggled for his last breath. I know suffocating is a horrible way to go. My poor mother and what she endured. She lost her soulmate and best friend. They did everything together. I shake my head.

"Oh, fuck," I shout. "My father just died. Alone."

"Oh, oh. I sorry ... so sorry."

"Fuck ... fuck ... fuck."

"I sorry. Here, here."

"Thanks. I'm sorry."

"It ..."

"Thanks for being here."

I stand up. I stare at CT's sympathetic eyes. She tilts my head down and kisses my mouth. It is a long kiss. She's trying to ease my pain. She does. Her kiss helps me recover. She blows more life into me; she increases my will to continue.

When CT's deep kiss finally ends, I say, "Oh, Dad."

I take her hand, and we walk over to the window and stare at the Naval Academy's Chapel. I'm not sure how long we stood there, but the entire time, we embraced.

At last, I turn to CT, "I'm so glad you're here. I don't want to be alone tonight. Can you stay with me?"

"Yes. I stay."

"Thank you. Thank you very much."

"We stay together."

"Good. I need you. I don't think I should be alone."

"It okay."

CT and I embrace, and we kiss another deep kiss. I hold my Vietnamese companion. My crying subsides. I keep thinking how sad my poor mother is feeling. Once Dad became sick, we both knew he might not recover. But, we weren't prepared for him to die—not so soon. Dying is final.

I'm barely able to function.

"Do you want to eat some more?"

"No, I put thing away."

"Thanks … thanks a lot. Whew, let me finish making our drinks. I'm so sorry you have to see me like this."

I raise my hands to my face. CT holds me. I'm such a mess. I'm falling apart.

"It okay. No problem."

Cam-Tu finds the storage containers and packs up our half-eaten dinner. She tidies up. I finish making our drinks. I give her a generous amount of Maker's Mark this time. After I blow my nose, we resettle on the couch.

I feel a terrible pain. I keep thinking I'll never hear my Dad's voice, see his smile, or hug him again. I keep thinking about his last breath ... my poor mother. They were so close and dependent on one another. It's going to be hard. I'm not sure I can get through this either. I feel angry with the Chinese ... the damn coronavirus.

For a while, Cam-Tu and I sip our drinks and hold hands without talking. Many thoughts race around in my head. I'm not able to control them. When a painful thought or memory enters my mind, I drink. I open up more and tell her about my family and childhood.

CT listens. She understands what I'm talking about. I ask about her parents. I can tell she wants to be sympathetic to my situation though, and not get into details about her father's death. I learn her Mom is alive and staying in Ho Chi Minh City in southern Vietnam. It helps me a great deal to talk about her family.

I make more drinks. CT is feeling the Maker's Mark. She's not a drinker. I lead her into the bedroom. I give her a towel and toothbrush. I brush my teeth. After her shower, a nude CT joins me in bed.

CHAPTER 25

I WAKE UP SUFFERING from a hangover. I look for the lovely Miss Nguyen, but she's gone. I rub my eyes. She left a note.

> Dear Doc,
>
> Thank you last night. I sorry you Dad die. Very, very sorry. When my dad die, I much young you. It break heart many piece. I not know how live without father. He import my life. I glad I with you last night. But, maybe, you regret thin. Thin we share. I understand. I want see you again. But, you feel otherwise? I understand. I treasure last night forever.
>
> Kiss and hug,
> CT
>
> PS. Email me camtunguyen25@gmail.com

I wonder what the hell happened. Regrets? No, I don't have any regrets. You helped me get through last night. All things considered, I slept well. I have no idea what time she left. I can't say if she would have stayed under different circumstances; that's a moot point. My father's death influenced our behaviors.

I feel soreness in my lower back, as I fetch a glass of water.

***

When my head clears, I send Cam-Tu an email explaining how happy I am that we spent the evening together. Based on her email address, she is probably late 20s. Our difference in ages doesn't bother me. Tom is twice as old as Joy. I wrote I want to see her again. She is a lovely companion. I'll write again, once I finish reading the Dean's paperwork.

I shouldn't be getting involved with anyone from the Naval Academy, but I'm not working there yet. And, the circumstances in which our relationship started were beyond control. I need her. She can prevent a total eclipse of my heart.

While trying to keep my mind off my father's tragic death, I return to *The Thai Wife Story Joy* … a writer must write.

CHAPTER 26

THE NAVY SEAL drifted back to his fateful September 11th. More than two months passed since then. Tom accepted those events more readily now. He has a purpose. Despite the pain and humiliation, the replaying of his final meeting with Dr. Jones assisted the healing process.

Tom feels lucky to have a boss like Dr. Jones. Although Tom knows his undercover status might land him some dirty jobs, he'll do whatever Cody believes is best. They trained Tom to follow orders. He trusts his boss.

The glass of Maker's Mark returned to Tom's lips, and he took a generous swallow. During his time in Thailand, he came to think of himself as Doc, rather than Tom. Psychologically, this change of persona helps him move on with his journey. The only one whom he really knows in Bangkok is Joy and to her, he is Doc.

The masseuses at Lucky Massage and ladyboy Bpee call him Doc. He told everyone whom he met to call him Doc. He never gives out his real name. While in Asia, he sees no reason to ever use his real name. Thailand has given him another opportunity.

Tom was fired by one of his father's understudies and best friends. It's a huge disgrace and embarrassment for him. Although he can never forget his great shame and disappointment from that day, he needed to progress from that event. His sexy Issarn masseuse provided a good distraction. The green-faced man promised himself that he would meet any forthcoming challenges head on. He recited part of the Navy SEAL's creed several times: "If knocked down, I will get back up, every time …"

After my father's tragic death, I too need to get back up and face my challenges. I hope that Cam-Tu can become my Joy.

Joy focused Tom's mind on love making and a simpler way of life. He began to feel comfortable in Thailand. His self-talk repeatedly stated that he wouldn't let Jones down. He wouldn't disappoint the memory of his father nor the United States of America. He wouldn't make any more mistakes. He would work hard, as a problem solver for his country.

The expression on Tom's face showed a serious determination. It was 1:30 PM. He planned to meet Ryan Daniels in exactly one hour. Tom departed to his arranged meeting place, wondering how it would go. He felt eager to meet Daniels. Tom expected to learn more details about his future.

Tom wanted to get his first assignment. He knew the Asia-Pacific Theater was busy. He believed that getting back to work would be good for him. He wanted to stay sharp, and being in the field is the best way. No matter how good training sessions or simulations are, they never approach the real thing. When training exercises go south, the consequences don't amount to much. In the real world, a mistake can be fatal.

Although Tom knew Joy for only two weeks, the intensity of their relationship and frequency of sex made it feel as if they'd been together far longer. She spent every recent night with him. He worries about the difficulty in saying good-bye to Joy, when he needs to depart for Chiang Mai.

Tom held out some hope that he would get to stay in Bangkok longer, or perhaps be granted permission to relocate his girlfriend to Chiang Mai. Maybe Joy wouldn't be allowed to come immediately, but perhaps once he got settled, she could follow. Tom was getting ahead of himself. He didn't like the thought of being apart from Joy.

***

Back in Fort Meade, Maryland, Dr. Cody Jones slept soundly. By the time he woke up, Tom and

Ryan already would have met in Bangkok. Jones expects Daniels or an assistant to provide an update about their meeting, and Tom's situation. The updates received so far about him indicated that he's adjusting well.

CHAPTER 27

VIA TAXI, THE NAVY SEAL made his way to the luxurious Bamboo Bar at the Mandarin Oriental Hotel. Although only five miles away, Bangkok's traffic lived up to its reputation, and the trip took almost an hour. Upon entering the bar, Tom saw a well-built Caucasian man sipping a drink. He realized the man was Ryan Daniels.

Undisguised Navy SEALs stand out like a sore thumb in Thailand. The key to achieving a successful and safe meeting is to pick a secure location with numerous options for a quick escape. Daniels chose the Bamboo Bar. Other than the staff and the man at the bar, the place was empty. So far, the arrangement looked good. Tom made a mental note of the exits. In their line of work, they can't risk a misstep.

Both Ryan and Tom intended to follow the agreed upon identity-verification protocol. They know all too well the details of Dave Kennedy and Brody Mitchell's tragic story involving mistaken identities and murder. Carelessness killed those two

Navy SEALs. Dr. Jones's reputation and the success of the cyber operations planned in the Asia-Pacific Theater hinged on everyone on their team making good decisions. Because Tom and Ryan never had met, they couldn't be too cautious, even in circumstances that appeared harmless.

Tom sat down in one of the pillow-cushioned bamboo chairs, and faced the bartender. The tiered display of spirits impressed Tom. The mirrored ceiling magnifies the large cache of liquor, making the plush room appear even grander. The colorful display and the variety of the bottles' shapes and sizes caused Tom's mouth to water. The taxi ride and Bangkok's climate contributed to his thirst.

Tom pulled out his agency phone, which although appearing like any standard mobile, is far from it. A waiter approached his table.

"Welcome to the Bamboo Bar, sir. This is our a-cappella cocktail menu. Do you need a minute, sir?"

"Nice shirt and tie."

"Thank you, sir."

The Navy SEAL glanced at the slate of specialty drinks.

"Nice menu, but I think I've decided."

"Please go ahead, sir."

Tom raised his voice so that the patron at the end of the bar could hear.

"I need a Maker's Mark and 7Up. It tastes expensive ... and is."

"Maker's Mark and 7Up."

"Make it a double."

"Yes, sir. I'll bring you some snacks too."

"Thanks."

The server hurried back to the bar. Tom texted Daniels at the number provided by Dr. Jones back at Fort Meade—Meet me at 2:30. A text from Daniels's number came back with Maker's Mark's tagline from the 1970s: "It tastes expensive … and is." Tom smiled on receiving the confirmation.

Tom texted back: "Manos arriba." On cue, the man at the end of the bar raised his hands. After saying something to the bartender in Thai, the man picked up his glass and walked over to Tom's table.

"Howdy. Been in Bangkok long?"

"About two weeks. You?"

"Two-thousand, five-hundred, and thirty-one days."

The man's number is the secret prime-number key that Tom expected; it confirmed his identity. The two Navy SEALs went old school with their authentications, but the clandestine nature of their operations requires them to leave *no* digital footprint that might look suspicious, even to the NSA.

Although the frogmen believe their agency phones are secure, they don't want to take any risks. They assume all text messages will be intercepted by adversaries and analyzed by AI programs. They also figure watchdog friendlies will intercept their messages. The SEALs use innocuous text messages that programs won't flag, as meriting a second level of scrutiny.

The SEALs worry that encrypted messages might trigger a red flag. Even though eavesdroppers can't decrypt such messages in real-time, sender locations could be determined. If discernible communication patterns persist, the SEALs know that agents might be dispatched to their location to investigate.

Tom stood up and extended his hand, "Tom …"

"I know who you are. The pleasure is all mine, sir."

Tom → "Thanks."

Ryan → "Thanks."

They shook hands firmly. Daniels held onto Tom's forearm. The two green-faced men stared into each other's eyes.

"Have a seat."

"Thanks."

The two compatriots smiled—one close brothers share after not having met for many years. While being overseas, it felt good to make contact with another American. The idea of getting back to work bolstered Tom's ego; he felt raring to go. Daniels projected a positive and cocky vibe that boosted Tom's confidence.

"Great to meet you finally. Cody thinks the world of you. He's sticking his neck out, brother.

Not just for you, but for me too. We're quite lucky to get this gig in Thailand."

"He's a great guy."

"Love him like a father."

"Me too. I'm very thankful. This is going to be some operation."

"Yeah, it is."

The server returned, set down a fancy coaster, and placed Tom's perspiring drink on top.

"Here you go, sir."

"Thanks. About those snacks you promised?"

"Coming right up, sir. Sorry, sir."

The server motioned to another staff member.

"Bring me a glass of ice please," Daniels requested.

"Right away, sir."

Another server approached. He set down a bowl of peanuts, and a second one containing snack mix.

"Thanks. This snack mix is pretty good. I've been munching on it at the bar."

A third server returned with Daniel's ice request. Tom grabbed a handful of the snack mix.

"Yeah, you're right. This stuff's tasty. This place isn't too shabby."

Tom reached for his glass and took a long drink. It went down smoothly.

"I love this place. Never draws a crowd. At least I've never seen one. I suppose during the celebration of the King's 60th year on the throne, it was packed. The prices are too high for locals. And, there usually aren't any good-looking women ... helps keep the spoiled brats away."

"Very laid back vibe. Library-like appearance. Can't say it puts me in a study mood. The selection of booze is outrageous."

"A lot of famous writers have stayed at this hotel over the years: Somerset Maugham, Joseph Conrad, Leo Tolstoy, Graham Greene, Victor ... Victor. What's that guy's last name?"

"Who?"

"Victor ... Victor ... you know the guy who wrote *The Hunchback of Notre Dame*?"

Tom scratched his head.

"I'll think of it. They pretty much have everything that you could ever want ... in terms of alcohol."

"I see that."

"Anything else, sir?"

Tom → "No."

Ryan → "No, we're fine for now."

"Service isn't too bad either."

"No, we've got like five people waiting on us."

"Amazing Thailand."

I feel a little offended that Daniels didn't mention my name in the list of authors who'd stayed at the Mandarin Oriental. After all, I won a Nobel Prize in literature, and certainly not everyone on his list had done that ... out of respect for the original author's decision, I decide not to add my name.

Daniels dropped a couple ice cubes in and took a big swallow. As the two chatted, they snacked. Tom looked around at the colorful bottles. The five-star bar impressed him. He thought it would be nice to spend a few nights at the hotel with Joy.

I decide to join the Navy SEALs and get up to fix myself a drink. I grab some wasabi almonds.

CHAPTER 28

*A*S I SIP MY *Maker's Mark, I think about Cam-Tu. She's a life saver. Without her support, I would have been very depressed. I worry about my Mom, and I write a post-it reminder to call. I stare out at the Naval Academy's Chapel ...*

After freshening up my drink, I return to the table. I find myself making fewer edits to this section. I'm now into JoyPart21. As you're aware from my annoyance at Daniels, I often stayed at the Mandarin. It previously ranked in the top-ten best hotels in the world. I rejoin Tom and Ryan at the Bamboo Bar.

"I've got eyes on you."

"I figured you probably did."

"You've found a real looker in little Joy."

Tom smiled. He hoped she never had serviced Ryan. Tom tried to convince himself that Ryan wouldn't go there. Daniels and his staff members probably had been watching from a distance. Tom hopes so. He hadn't picked up on any surveillance.

There is ladyboy Bpee, but until now, it never occurred to Tom that she could be working for Daniels. Other than Bpee, there is only that other Thai masseuse who propositions him along Su-khumvit. Tom thought about it carefully. Perhaps she is working for Daniels. Tom needs to improve his situational awareness.

Tom knows the NSA can track anyone, any-where, at any time, and without being detected. Daniels is aware of Tom's every move. If giving up personal privacy is part of the sacrifice needed to help save American lives, Tom is willing to make that sacrifice. Dr. Jones and Ryan feel the same way. Tom knows he's in excellent company.

"Joy's really a nice girl."

"Great cover for you."

Daniels smiled. He almost added, "Don't get too attached," but he knows Tom passed that point. Daniels has a long history with Thai women, and he enjoys the fringe benefits associated with working in Thailand. Tom took a gulp.

"God, that's good."

"I heard from Cody you like to drink."

Daniels plopped in another ice cube.

"We all have our vices, I suppose."

"Yes, we do."

"Thanks for understanding."

Tom raised his glass. The green-faced men toasted. Daniels adopted a more serious tone.

"You're to move up to Chiang Mai in about a week. The city's crawling with Chinese. About a week after you get there, a Chinese hacker who works out of the Pudong New Area in Unit 61398 for the People's Liberation Army will be arriving in Chiang Mai. Our intelligence indicates his handle is 'Ugly Gorilla.' You can read more about him in one of Mandiant's reports. They're actually available online. Look for APT1 ..."

Ryan → "Advanced Persistent Threat One."

Tom → "Advanced Persistent Threat One."

The Navy SEALs laughed.

"We're planning to give Ugly Gorilla a laptop," Daniels put air quotes around the word 'give,' and continued, "On that laptop will be a malicious CC client. If Ugly Gorilla takes it back to his Shanghai headquarters and boots up, as we anticipate, he'll unknowingly set up a digital beachhead for us right there in the middle of Chinese cyber operations."

"Brilliant. Sounds like an awesome plan."

"We're still ironing out the finer points. Ugly Gorilla's wife doesn't want him to travel to Chiang Mai without her. She's jealous of beautiful Chiang Mai women. Our intelligence is that she's close to convincing him she needs to tag along. We might be able to make use of her. The more distracted Ugly Gorilla is, the better our chances."

Tom thought about Joy's comments on Chiang Mai's women. Apparently, their beauty is internationally known. Tom imagined that a guy named,

Ugly Gorilla, doesn't pick up a lot of women based on his good looks.

"How do you guys dig this shit up?"

"Well, you know . . . In fact, I think we used some of your software."

Ryan slapped Tom on the back.

"Ha, ha, ha."

"If we go green, I'll be getting an infected laptop to you … you'll arrange for it to fall into Ugly Gorilla's hands."

"Clever. A guy like that—I'm sure his curiosity will get the best of him."

"Yeah, we're counting on it. For now, that's everything I have. I'll be in touch with the rest."

"I'll make my way up to Chiang Mai in about a week then."

"We know where to find you."

Ryan smiled and placed his phone on the table. His phone appears identical to the one Jones gave Tom in September.

"Use only this phone for business. Never use it to call anyone, except me or Cody."

"Understood."

"Never use it to send any messages that could be mined for intel."

"Got it."

"If anything happens. I mean if you get compromised, don't let it fall into the wrong hands. There's a tracking chip that reports back to one of our servers. Typing the binary code for 28 and calling detonates the phone in five seconds. You don't want to be near it when it blows.

"As a last resort, it can be used as a grenade à la James Bond, to save your ass. Ha, ha, ha. Only as a last resort. Ha, ha."

"You serious?"

"Totally."

"Jeez, I guess up until this point you figured I wouldn't be dialing that number on my own."

"Ha, ha, ha. Boom, boom. Yeah, we took that chance. It wasn't a big risk. We knew you wouldn't be doing anything, except for communicating with us. Keep it secure at all times."

Tom laughed and smiled. Daniels laughed and stirred his drink.

"I will, and more so now than ever. I won't be carrying it in my front pocket either. Ha, ha."

The two men continued laughing and shaking their heads. Only a green-faced man could find humor in learning that he'd been carrying a bomb around in his front pocket, with the possibility of accidently blowing up his family jewels.

Finally, after a lot of back slapping and toasting, they regained composure.

"Okay, 1-1-1-0-0. Then we have a Samsung-battery problem."

"Ka-boom, but on a bigger scale. Yeah, right. No evidence. Ha, ha, ha."

"Ha, ha, ha."

"Hugo … Victor Hugo."

"What?"

"He wrote *The Hunchback of Notre Dame.*"

CHAPTER 29

I FIX MYSELF *another drink, so I can join the* SEALs *in a final toast. Daniels continues.*

"In Thailand, I've got access to damn-near anything you need. All untraceable. I'm practically a warehouse—computers, surveillance cameras, recording devices and mics, software back doors ... viruses, worms, Trojan horses, even some zero days. Custom versions of our internal packet-monitoring software, bank accounts, password-cracking programs, a remote tool for accessing calls or messages on someone else's phone, hacker's toolkit ... uhh, jamming devices that turn security cameras black, command-and-control-center thumb drives ... I've basically got whatever Cody has available back home. Well, not quite."

"Impressive."

"When you need real firepower ... sniper rifles, handguns, ammunition, smoke, and grenades."

"I've got one grenade already."

"Ha, ha. Night-vision googles, vests, diving gear, knives … everything's untraceable. Take a set, carbon-fiber brass knuckles. Umm, I know that's an oxymoron."

"Cool, thanks. Light."

"We've got an excellent forger. Several programmers, not in your league though. Decoys and assistants—a few real lookers too. Cleaners, and even cops on payroll. They can fix a scene. Keep you out of harm's way. This place is so corrupt. Comes in real handy."

"Great, you've built up an incredible team."

"You'd be surprised. I'm forgetting something. Ah, I've got damn near anything you can ever need. Well, almost anything. I would, of course, need advance notice in some cases, bro."

Tom appreciated Daniels's sense of humor, and his SEAL brother's effort to make light of what could turn out to be a dangerous, and perhaps deadly, game.

"Can you get me a new phone if I blow this one? Assuming I'm still alive."

"Ha, ha, ha. Yeah, we can. We can get a new one, right away. Don't hesitate to blow that one. Ha, ha."

"On the flights over, I didn't have any problem getting through security."

"Yeah, you won't. It goes through undetected."

"Okay."

"Always leave it on, even while flying."

"Roger that."

"There's a special receiver. We might need to get you an urgent message."

"Seems like you've got everything covered."

"Everything except boom, boom. Ha, ha, ha. But, I see you're having no trouble finding that on your own, brother. Bangkok does that to yah. There's a reason foreigners pronounce it, 'bang cock.' Stay safe."

Daniels slapped Tom on the back. Tom burped and smiled. He felt good to be back in the game. Daniels picked out a few pretzels. Tom finished the peanuts and washed them down with Maker's.

"Thanks. I guess we're good to go. Appreciate your help on this. I feel better already."

"We're all in this together."

They raised their glasses.

"Cheers, here's to our success."

"To our success."

I raise my glass to join the green-faced men, and say out loud, "To our success. Good luck, boys. Wishing you the best."

"Check in with me from time-to-time. The usual bland text will suffice. We're sure these phones are secure, but let's keep communication to a minimum anyway."

"Gotcha."

"Hang loose. When I've got more details on the Chiang Mai op, I'll message—details about laptop delivery, drop off, and so on. I can get things to you easily."

"Thanks. Thanks a lot," Tom added with feeling.

They finished their drinks. Tom licked his lips. The distinguished SEAL had been disgraced back at Fort Meade, but he'd been given a chance at redemption. With the help of Ryan and Cody, Tom intends to restore his name.

"I'll take care of this."

Daniels motioned for the bill.

"Once you've been in Chiang Mai for a while, open yourself a savings account on campus at the Chiang Mai University Branch of SIAM Commercial Bank. Get an ATM card. Use cash for all transactions."

"Sure."

"Send me your account number, and I'll make you a millionaire. Ha, ha, ha."

"Sounds good. Sounds better than good."

"Hang out at the university. Meet some people there. Blend in. Maybe enroll in some Thai lessons, or tutor English on a volunteer basis. Good way to meet some jail bait. Get involved with whatever floats your boat. The distraction will provide good cover."

"Will do."

"Here take this," Daniels handed Tom a wad of cash, "This should hold you. Best of luck, frogman."

"Thanks, you too, brother. Hooyah."

"Hooyah."

With their exchange complete, they shook hands—the way only two green-faced men can. They'd been through the same training and are in the same brotherhood. The Navy SEALs bond similarly to climbers. If one man makes a mistake, both die. They take responsibility for each other's back, and they give one another complete trust.

While Daniels remained settling the bill, Tom left. He didn't look back. He is always being watched. Tom shook his head and grinned, as he went through the hotel's opulent lobby. The idea isn't for him to be invisible, but rather for him to blend in—just another farang looking for love.

Tom glanced up at the giant chandelier, looked around at the security cameras and the guards, and headed out the lobby's main entrance.

"Need a cab, sir?" a bellhop asked.

"Not today thanks. I prefer walking."

"Yes, sir."

The bell cap saluted. Instinctively, Tom went to salute, but caught himself. He left the hotel's security behind. He walked away from the Chao Phraya River, up a small soi to Charoen Krung 40 Alley. So far, in the steamy south Asian country, things had gone to plan. He's enjoying himself far more than he would have been back in Anne Arundel County.

The Navy SEAL thought about what a great guy Dr. Jones is. As a team, they're going to secure

America's interests and national security. Tom feels grateful he's been given a role to keep Americans safe and free. He likes Daniels a lot already, and Tom knows they'll work well together.

"Tuk-tuk?" a small Thai man begged.

The driver interrupted Tom's train of thought.

"Mai krap."

"You speak Thai wery well," the driver said in clear English.

The American couldn't help but smile. He'd spoken only two words in Thai, but the driver complemented him on his language ability. Compliments are paid out more freely on the streets of Bangkok than during BUD/S training.

Tom recalled one time sitting and facing the cold, breaking Pacific surf for ten hours on a beach near Coronado. While locked in each other's arms, the prospective SEALs had been called 'piss ants.' The compliment given to those who didn't pass out or quit was, 'Not bad, ladies.' Halfway around the world, an entirely different culture and set of standards govern.

Small Thai man 1 → "Tuk-tuk?"

Small Thai man 2 → "Where you go?"

Small Thai man 3 → "Me have lady."

Tom ignored the annoying tuk-tuk drivers. Although the three Thai guys heard the American turn down the previous driver, Bangkok forced them to try their luck. The uneducated Issarn drivers barely eke out a living. Their meager income depends on whether farangs are in the mood to walk or ride. Tom passed several impressive displays of silver and antiques, before turning onto a larger road.

The smells emanating from the polluted and backed-up drains almost made the hardened Navy SEAL wretch. Even in broad daylight, packs of rats run in and out of sewers; they hide among big plastic garbage bags on the streets. Tom noticed Thai people slurping bowls of piping-hot noodles. The smells that made him sick didn't seem to bother them.

In front of a small restaurant, skinned ducks, hanging by their necks in a filthy glass display case, caught the American's eye. Tom and his team members are sticking their necks out too, and he prayed for the safety of everyone involved. He wondered how long the ducks had been hanging there, and if he would get sick, if he ate one. He took a pass.

Tom sped up, as thoughts of meeting Joy flooded his mind. The Issarn masseuse always satisfied him, and she always came on time.

CHAPTER 30

JOY SLEPT AT TOM'S room. They tried to spend as much time together as possible, because in two days, he would depart for Chiang Mai. He loved his silent alarm; his little bundle of joy got him up quickly. Whenever she spent the night, his morning was filled with delight.

He'd been in Bangkok for almost three weeks. Despite the days flying past, his time with Joy made him feel younger. He raised his arm. She rolled over and stared. He gazed into her lovely big eyes.

"Good morning, baby."

"He, he, he. Me wery happy, babe."

Even at their first meeting, Tom had called Joy 'baby.' When talking to his lover now, he used that word exclusively. She called him 'babe.' His love for Joy is one he never expected. He learned a lot about life from observing her simple behavior.

Joy loves her American boyfriend. She accepts everything about him, and she never asks any questions about his past. Without saying it, she said, "No matter what you are, I'll always be with you."

Bangkok wipes the slate of every newcomer clean. The past doesn't exist. People live in the moment. Their relationship possesses a purity. The present, and one or two days into the future are all that matter.

"Here, baby, I picked this up for you."

"Oh, you sweet ka."

"Thanks."

"Ka."

He watched Joy unwrap the unexpected gift. When she saw the Victoria's Secret perfume, she shed a tear. With great innocence, she sprayed a mist from the winged bottle onto her wrists. She sprayed some over the bed too. They both smelled the expensive fragrance.

"Good smell ka. Thank you, babe. You wery good man, babe."

"I'm so glad you like it, baby."

"Me never have Wictoria Secret ka."

"You do now. You do now, baby."

"Ka. You wery sweet, babe."

"Thanks."

"Ka."

A chasm exists between their education levels. Joy's natural ability exceeds the average, but her schooling ended in the sixth grade. Tom ranked first in his graduating class. He completed many advanced courses, as part of his work at the NSA. While working there, he pushed his mental limits and conducted complex research with teams of brilliant mathematicians and computer scientists. He worked on the cutting edge of cybersecurity—finding vulnerabilities in complex software systems and developing exploits to take advantage of those bugs.

Joy had been instructed that she didn't need an education. She'd been discouraged from using her mind, but instead encouraged to use her body. Sometimes, she doesn't possess the knowledge to perform a straightforward task. Her lack of education means she possesses little curiosity and few critical-thinking skills. Sadly, she doesn't have the capability of wondering about most things—her dreams are limited. Tom wants to know how everything works, and he loves taking things apart. He enjoys talking about any subject; he wants to learn new things.

One compartment of his brain contains a library. There is a huge section devoted to computing and technology. He also loves history, particularly military history. Joy simply reacts to whatever situation comes her way. She relies on her street smarts. He plans many things, using his vast knowledge and experience. Her spontaneity is fun.

Thai versus American culture plays a big role in the lovers' differences. Age is another factor. Other than learning how to please a customer, Joy's knowledge has increased little since the age of 12. Tom continues to develop himself intellectually, always moving on to more involved subject matter. He steadily adds more volumes to his library.

Joy never traveled outside Thailand, and she hasn't traveled hardly at all inside it either. The American already knows the names and locations of the provinces better than Joy. She only seems to care about where she is at any given moment. Joy devotes herself to work and supporting her family. She doesn't have any hobbies.

Because his work is top secret, he can't talk about it. Due to her lack of curiosity, he never has the urge to explain anything about his background. She never asked. It's as though she said, "No matter what you do, I'll always be with you." They're highly compatible.

The uneducated Issarn girl can't make informed decisions about most topics. However, in some strange way, there's a richness and freshness to Joy. She accepts her circumstance, has a positive outlook, and expresses few needs that aren't sexual or material. She has no hang-ups; she respects all people; she's generous. Her admirable traits stem from her Buddhist upbringing and village customs.

Tom wonders whether Joy possessing the ability to think critically would spoil her contentedness and beauty. Not having problem-solving ability, she doesn't analyze things, and that innocence provides her with a freedom from worry and responsibility.

She has no basis to pass judgments; she accepts everything at face value.

She can't play mind games, and she doesn't put up walls. Only in the sexual domain can she apply cunning, deception, and critical-thinking skills. Experience and the shop girls taught Joy much. She reached a level of expertise where she can serve as an instructor to other girls, giving hands-on lessons.

I laugh.

Although highly skilled in a particular type of manual labor, the same couldn't be said of her mastery of other subjects. It isn't as though she can't learn, but she has never been given the opportunity. People in high-ranking positions in the country who understand that education causes freedom of thought prefer to keep the masses in the dark.

***

Tom's lower back ached from their intense session from the previous evening. He felt soreness in his knees. As a trained Navy SEAL, if he was getting sore, he wondered what doll-like Joy felt. Her wrists bothered her from his-favorite position. Her skin never bruised.

Joy never complains. Her ability to derive pleasure from pain amazes Tom. He knows several Navy SEALs whose pain thresholds are lower than hers. She comes more times than any woman whom he'd ever met. He doesn't plan on telling anyone about Joy; no one would believe him anyway.

Tom loves hanging out with Joy. In her world, he ignores responsibility and lives freely. Bangkok leads people down that path. He adapted to her lifestyle, and this life freed him from the chains of the Western world.

CHAPTER 31

JOY FELT THE LOVE the American possesses for her. She understands love, caring, and kindness. The young Thai girl's feeling of guilt led to her confession that morning.

"Babe, Joy sorry you ka. Joy lie you. Me not weally wirgin ka," she said downheartedly.

Her touching confession and self-reproach caused heartache in the Navy SEAL. She broke down in tears. She doesn't cry often. His compassion poured forth, and he reached an arm around, pulled her close, and hugged her. She trembled, and he tried to comfort her.

Tom hadn't thought about Joy's virginity, but he knows no virgin can perform as skillfully as she does. Unlike men from certain cultures, he prefers her sexual talents to virginity. Given her upbringing, she couldn't comprehend such a preference. He never attempted to explain it. She makes generalizations based on a single observation. If one man prefers a virgin, then all men do, regardless of extenuating circumstances.

"That's okay, baby."

"Me bad girl. Me lie you ka. Me wery sorry. Wery, wery sorry."

"Baby, I understand. It's okay. Bangkok made you lie. Things will be all right. I don't mind."

"Mai sure."

"Really, baby."

"Ka."

He squeezed her warmly. She shivered. The anchor of lost virginity nearly drowned the poor teenager. In her village, men only married women whom they thought were virgins. Joy worried he would leave her. She bit a nail. Her mind went blank.

I wonder how you tell a woman is a virgin. I move my thumb off my chin and drink some Maker's Mark. I hope their relationship isn't coming to an end. Although a warrior, Tom seems like a compassionate man.

The contradictions in Thai society caused by class distinctions, interactions with foreigners, and age-old customs aren't reconciled easily.

"Me wery sad ka."

"Baby, it's okay."

"Me sad ka."

"Oh, baby. Don't cry."

"Ka."

Joy raised her hands and cupped her face. Her head drooped. Tom never had seen her depressed.

He downplayed his travel plans and provided reassurance. To Joy, Chiang Mai is on the other side of the world. She never flew. If you couldn't get there by motorbike or tuk-tuk, you couldn't get there at all.

Joy feared her revelation would cause the American to abandon her. She mistakenly applied the norms of a Thai man to him. She experienced terrible guilt. For the first time in her life, she thought about the future. The unknown caused deep anxiety.

"You go Chiang Mai two day ka. Joy want virgin for you, babe. No one come behind ka. That for you ka."

"Baby ..."

"Ka. Me sure."

"Oh."

"Ka."

Startled by Joy's offer, Tom realized how important virginity is to her, how much she cares for him, and how special their relationship is. He injured several past girlfriends. Those women are much larger. One actress who offered herself to him threatened a lawsuit. Joy loves him. She'll do anything to try and keep him.

Joy could see he was hesitating. She cracked her knuckles. She felt confused, and his indecisiveness lowered her confidence and self-esteem. She offered the last part of her purity to him. It looked as if he was rejecting it. It broke Tom's heart to see her distraught and vulnerable. He wiped away her tears.

CHAPTER 32

AFTER SAYING good-bye to ladyboy Bpee, Tom released his grip on Joy's hair. The images of Bpee's anatomy trouble him far less now than they had just a couple weeks ago. Joy limped to the bathroom. When Tom heard the water running, he stood up. He joined her in the shower.

They took turns washing. She used a sponge. He avoided touching her behind. They washed Joy's messy hair. She massaged his head. He felt the warm water cleanse him. For Joy, the act cleared her conscience for having lied to him.

"Here, towel ka."

"Thanks, baby."

They dried off together. Tom helped her with the blow dryer.

"Joy neck hurt ka."

"Sorry, baby. I think I choked you."

"Joy voice funny ka."

"You'll sound normal soon, baby. Like a sore throat. We'll get you cough drops."

"Me okay ka."

"I guess ... I lost it. At least for a moment ... or two. When I was thinking of her finishing in my ...," he caught himself. "I'm so glad that you're okay, baby. Sorry."

Tom swallowed. He readjusted himself. She didn't notice his red face.

"Ka."

Although she had no idea what he meant, she smiled. He became accustomed to her saying 'ka,' whenever she doesn't understand.

They laid down on the bed; he held her. His feelings came through. Joy felt secure. Exhaustion caused by trauma, blood loss, and repeated orgasming defeated her. She dozed off. He stared at his little Thai angel.

Time flew by when Tom was with Joy. These few weeks disappeared. Before he left for Chiang Mai, they planned to go sightseeing to celebrate. He wanted to share the city's tourist attractions, as the poor masseuse never had gone anywhere. He hoped she'd be able to walk.

Joy's virginity is completely gone. No matter what transpires, he'll live on in her memory, as the man to whom she gave the last part of her innocence. Still holding his darling little Thai masseuse, he closed his eyes and joined her in a blissful place.

***

I'm getting close to the end. I assume Tom will propose to Joy. If they marry, I know he'll be in for a few surprises. Although I never married, I figure everyone goes into marriage facing unknowns. She's proven her dedication. If he asks the big question, I think she'll respond 'yes.' No point in me speculating. In a couple months, Joy will probably find out she's pregnant. A while later she'll tell him. I say out loud, "Good luck, ole boy."

CHAPTER 33

DURING THE couple's penultimate evening, they ate at the Rib Room Restaurant at the Landmark Hotel on Sukhumvit. The American prefers Western food more than his young Issarn girlfriend does. He never feels full after eating Thai food. Noodles, rice, vegetables, and small portions that fill her make him hungrier. Farang food tastes bland to Joy, and she prefers spicy Issarn food.

Joy is starving. A formal setting normally makes her feel uncomfortable, but because a number of Thai-farang couples were eating there, she felt at ease. Tom gave her reassurances.

Joy enjoyed the views from the 31st floor. She never had been up that high. Throughout the meal, he could see her shifting in her chair to try and alleviate discomfort, but she never complained. After dinner, they took the lift to the Rendezvous Bar in the lobby. This time the lift didn't scare her.

Tom ordered drinks. When she accompanied him, the staff never ID'd her. After drinks, they grabbed a tuk-tuk back. After getting undressed, they fell asleep in each other's arms. Joy dreamt of marrying the American, and he dreamt of Bpee.

Tom woke up before Joy. Since he wanted her to sleep in, he decided to pack for the next day's trip to Chiang Mai. She planned to take the day off, so they could tour Bangkok. Saying good-bye would be difficult. And, if she asked him when he would return, he didn't have a good answer. It would depend on many things, unknowns that were out of his control.

As he arranged belongings, Tom reflected on how quickly they bonded. Joy made a great companion. He thought about his former lovers. In the states, women give him an elevated status because he is an Annapolis grad and a Navy SEAL, but his young Thai girl doesn't even know about those things.

Joy initially lied about her virginity, but later rectified things. Tom lies about being a doctor. His identity in Thailand morphed into that lie, and he doesn't know when he can come clean, if ever. He doesn't feel the white lie matters. It's working well. If she learned he isn't a doctor, it wouldn't have bothered her. She doesn't even really know what a doctor is, or how much schooling and training are needed to become one. Her understanding is someone who aids sick people and is smart.

Many questions floated around in the Navy SEAL's mind. Should he propose to Joy? Is she pregnant? What if she gives birth? Will their relationship last? Will the distance between Bangkok and Chiang Mai keep them apart? What is her family like?

Once he left Bangkok would she give happy endings to other customers? Would she engage in sex? Would she orgasm? Would she have unprotected sex? What would happen with their great sex life?

He possessed no satisfactory answers. When he dropped his suitcases near the door, she woke up.

"Morning, sleeping beauty."

"Morning ka."

"You're so cute when you rub your eyes. How do you feel, baby?"

"Pain here. Neck wery sore ka."

"Oh, baby, I'm sorry."

"Me okay ka."

Joy dragged her tired body out of bed. Her gait showed extreme discomfort.

"When you're ready, baby, we'll explore Bangkok."

"Farang know Bangkok better me ka. Never go out."

"Today you will, Joy. I'm going to take you around the city."

"He, he, he. You sweet man ka."

"I want you to see some of Thailand's capital."

"Ka."

She showered, dressed, and put on makeup. He splashed on cologne and reviewed his notes.

"Baby, today you wear sandals. You'll be on your feet a lot. Probably walk more than ever before."

"On your feet lot?"

"Walking. We walk much today. Very far."

"Oh. Okay ka."

"I know Thai people don't like to walk in the heat."

"Ka. Me okay, babe."

"Okay, good."

Joy's sandals show off her sexy feet. He knew she would be sore while walking around, but her virginity offering wasn't something he anticipated. She took a drink and came over to him. During their kiss, she spit water into his mouth.

If they were going to make it out of the bedroom, he knew they needed to keep moving.

"You ready, baby?"

"Ka, babe."

"We'll take a taxi to Saphan Taksin. Hire a longtail boat there. Go for a private tour on the Chao Phraya River and canals."

"Joy never been boat. No swim ka."

"Don't worry. It'll be fun, baby. I'm a good swimmer and will take care of you."

"Love you ka."

"After our boat trip, we'll head to Chinatown. Then a few other places. See, I've written down this plan."

He held up his scribbles.

"You geng mahk ka."

Joy pretended to read his notes and express interest. He smiled and hugged her. He wants to lead, and she wants to follow.

Joy felt sentimental about her boyfriend's departure. She worried that once he left Bangkok, she would never see him again. She worries about the beautiful women in Chiang Mai. Tom definitely wants to see her again. Because she'd been lied to in the past, it's hard for her to accept his reassurances. Doubt lodged in her mind.

Tom refrained from telling Joy that he loves her. The words would have flowed naturally and honestly. He wants to say them. Several times, the words almost spilled out. He feels close to committing. He goes back and forth about proposing. As a Navy SEAL, he's been trained to make decisions.

Tom took both of Joy's hands, pulled her close to him, and kissed her with deep affection.

"Joy, I have something to ask you."

CHAPTER 34

I SPENT CONSIDERABLE time on the phone with my mother over the past few days. I tried my best to console her, but there wasn't much I could say. I hope sharing phone time will give her more strength. I know it does me. My Dad is to be cremated, and eventually, the ashes will reach me.

My Dad's will makes his last wishes clear; he designed things to minimize the burden on us. He was a thoughtful and kind person—a really great guy. He had a good sense of humor. I would give everything I own to have him back again. My Mom misses her soulmate, best friend, and life-long companion. The coronavirus keeps us apart.

My parents accumulated close to 100-million dollars in various accounts and investments. As an only child, I'll need to manage their life savings for my mother. During the next few weeks, she'll be sending me accounts, passwords, phone numbers for attorneys, and more. My Mom's health has been good, but I worry about her. She still goes outdoors to exercise. With each passing day, I sense her will to live decreases. My over-the-phone efforts have failed to reverse this awful trend.

Cam-Tu visits regularly, and we get along well. We fill a gap in each other's life. She came along at a perfect time. Given that she spends most of her time in isolation, I must have been there at the right time. I find Cam-Tu an interesting young lady, and she has taught me a lot about Vietnam. I feel badly about my misunderstandings of that country and its people.

Cam-Tu and I usually eat delivered dinners at my place, and afterwards, she spends the night. She's in the habit of bringing an overnight bag. If she asks, I'll let her store things here. CT has good instincts. Due to the restrictions imposed by the coronavirus, few people see her coming or going.

After one visit, I sent the paperwork back to the Academy to make my sabbatical official. The Dean wrote up a draft of a blurb to announce my starting delay. He crafted a nice article, and I gave him a few suggestions. When I saw the article online in the Capital Gazette and the Baltimore Sun, it flowed well. The article pretty much directed blame at the coronavirus and internal Navy issues. The Navy focuses on fired captains and other major problems on ships, rather than my professorship. I'm sure most readers simply glossed over my news.

China's power grab and handling of the coronavirus occupies the minds of many in government.

There are more important issues facing most people in the country than my situation. Tension has built to an extreme level due to fear, rising unemployment, and people's inability to relate to one another. I know that a single racial incident can spiral wildly out-of-control and lead to national demonstrations and protests. I pray nothing such as that occurs.

The depression caused by my father's death and my Mom's mental state is added to by the fact that Tom will be leaving for Chiang Mai soon. I imagine the emotional strain that Joy will soon be facing alone.

Some days, I find myself struggling to get back to work. I try to delay Tom's departure. Maybe my excessive drinking is a factor too. I made some progress, and I do want to tour Bangkok with the young couple ... that will be fun ... writing is hard work.

CHAPTER 35

THE SEXY LITTLE Thai girl and the handsome Navy SEAL got lucky with Bangkok's legendary traffic. They made good time and around 10 AM, reached the Sathon District's busy Silom Line BTS Skytrain station named Saphan Taksin. The Bangkok Mass Transit System moves hordes around the crowded city for a cheap fare. Many passengers flowed out of the concrete station.

Joy exited the backseat of the cramped, metered taxi first. Tom handed the driver a 100-baht bill for a 70-baht fare. The driver paused, fiddled busily in his pockets, and delayed their departure, by pretending not to have any change. Once he realized he'd won, he smiled. Although the change meant little to Tom, it represented another can of beer for the driver.

Joy grabbed Tom's hand, and he followed behind toward the pier at Taksin Bridge. The increased humidity near the river's edge slapped the couple rudely in their faces. The scene reminded

Tom of their first meeting. That meeting, triggered by her sweet voice and chase, confirmed Bangkok's ability to manipulate its residents.

Tom never dreamed they would be in a relationship. The poor Issarn girl hoped they would be, but her life would go on either way. Joy lives day-to-day in the capricious city. Like many Thais, she believes in destiny. If she hadn't received that phone call back at the room, Tom would have proposed.

"Over there, babe."

"I see."

"Ka."

They walked to a scrawny Thai man selling boat-ride tickets. His dirty white T-shirt indicated he doesn't have access to running water.

"Boat krap. You need boat, Mister?"

"Yes, for the two of us ... Private tour."

"Three hours, nine-hundred baht. You okay?"

The American sensed an inflated price and consulted his little Thai sweetheart. She confronted the Thai seller.

"Tam mai pang mahk?"

The ticket salesman stared angrily at the Issarn girl, as though she'd betrayed a fellow countryman.

"Joy say, 'why wery expensive?' "

"Okay, we'll find another. Lots of boats here. See."

"Ka."

Tom nodded. As the lovers left, the man hurried after them. Tom noticed a huge sweat ring around the man's collar. It was then that Bangkok's suffocating heat and humidity dealt Tom another vicious combination. Joy shielded her eyes from the sun.

"You first customer today, Mister. For you special, only seven-hundred baht. You okay?"

Tom consulted Joy. Because she doesn't know if that's fair, she simply nodded in approval. Tom had seen other tourists leaving in long-tail boats from near where the man was selling tickets, so he didn't really understand how they could be the first customers. He chalked it up to the Thai way of counting.

The seller won because Bangkok wears out any foreigner haggling with a Thai in the heat.

"Okay, fine."

"Krap."

"Ka."

Tom wanted to get Joy off her feet as quickly as possible.

"Ticket here. Boat there."

The man jerked his head in the direction of the boat.

"Ka."

Tom pulled out a 1,000 baht note.

"Have small money?"

"No. Only one thousand."

"Uh."

The seller frowned because he would have to get change. The role reversal from begging for business to returning money flipped the seller's attitude and status completely.

"Wait me krap."

"Ka."

"Okay."

As the seller headed off, Tom hoped they would see the ragged fellow again. While holding hands, they watched, as he raced from vendor to vendor. A few middle-aged farang women stared and shook their heads from side-to-side in disapproval of the young lovers. Joy smiled at them. One woman thought about what it would be like to have the handsome man on top of her. She smiled.

The sweaty ticket man returned and handed over the tickets and change.

"You go there, Mister. Get boat."

"Ruea dang?"

"Krap."

"Ka."

"Bye."

"Good-bye."

As they walked away to board their long-tail boat, the man called to lure his next customer.

"Boat rent! Cheap price! Scenic river trip. Boat rent ..."

Although disappointed about no tip, the boat man abruptly returned to his seller role. A few other shouting Thai men competed with him. A loud voice and persistence earns you money in Thailand.

"Glad I'm not doing that."

"Ka."

"You understand me, babe."

"Ka."

They walked toward the dock. Food vendors and tourists crammed into the area. Although the river smelled foul to Tom, Joy didn't notice anything. None of the Thais did. The Saphan Taksin pier buzzed with activity. Whenever a tourist approached closely, birds scattered.

I saw recent pictures of Bangkok, and these areas are deserted due to the coronavirus. Their severe lockdown continues. They fare better than the USA, at least according to the numbers in the news. Many of their cases are from workers returning from the Middle East. The bulk of the other cases are in Muslim areas in the south. They have problems with infected people crossing the porous borders illegally, especially from Myanmar and Laos.

I don't have credible information to judge if the numbers, coming out of Asia, are accurate. Some world leaders claim the numbers are phony. Thailand was the second country to report a case of COVID-19. It came from a Chinese tourist. With the Thai economy's heavy reliance on tourism, the government wants to get the country re-opened and running. In the back of my mind, I realize something else may be afoot, in the form of a power grab by the country's elite.

I can't imagine a quiet and non-chaotic Bangkok.

CHAPTER 36

A MAN WITH AN outstretched hand said, "Ticket."

"Here you are."

"Thanks, Boss."

"Bye."

"Ka."

"Good-bye."

Joy and Tom climbed onto the brightly colored and tippy long-tail boat.

"Watch head krap."

"Ka. Look here, babe."

"Thanks."

"Walk middle krap. Stay middle. Glang krap."

"You okay, Joy?"

"Ka."

"Okay, careful."

"Ka."

Their driver was a thin Thai geezer. His dark and grizzly skin is charred from too-much time in the sun. The wrinkles combined with his white hair add 15 years to his weathered appearance. The narrow boat swayed, and it challenged the lovers to reach their seats—wooden slats resting on the floor.

Joy feared falling in, and she gripped Tom's hand. When they sat down on the rotting wood, she breathed a sigh. Their buttocks were raised but a few inches off the deck. He positioned himself directly behind her. Both turned to watch the geezer trying to start the rusty engine.

After several vigorous pulls on the fraying cord, a black cloud appeared, and the engine roared. The smoke billowed into the boat operator's lungs, triggering a hacking cough that would last throughout their journey. Fortunately, for the two passengers, the wind carried the black smoke away, in the opposite direction of their perches.

Along the boat's bottom, Tom's legs wrapped around Joy. He placed his hands onto her lap. Her hands went on top. Once onto the wavy Chao Phraya River, she tensed up. Beneath her long hair, Joy's shoulders crept up to her ears. She let go of one of his hands and clutched the boat's side.

Mist from the waves snuck past the rigged plastic shields and wet the couple. The canoe-width boat pitched and rolled in the hot breeze, especially when they approached ferries. Tom wondered if the keel is the rusting pipe to which the propeller is attached. Joy continued gripping the rotting wood.

"It's okay, baby. You're fine."

Joy didn't speak. She leaned back into her muscular American for security. The boat headed upstream. Half the boats weren't sea worthy. Tom saw holes patched with plastic and small pieces of wood. The unsafe situation appalled him. Boats traveled haphazardly, and there were near misses. Most people in Thailand can't swim. So, whenever there is an accident, people drown.

Few boats have the standard safety equipment that is mandatory in most countries. As a Navy SEAL, Tom enjoyed the chaos and craziness of the water traffic. He hoped Joy would get more comfortable, as the trip progressed. Bangkok drained her energy.

Before too long, the boat passed the Mandarin Oriental Hotel, which Tom recognized. Joy never had seen it. He reflected on his Bamboo Bar meeting there with Ryan. From the river, one can see the rooms have spacious balconies.

Tom noticed the Mandarin operates its own water taxis. Those safer passenger ferries cross the river to reach the hotel's luxury spa. He wondered if the upscale massage parlors also offer happy endings. His buddies couldn't afford such places. Joy started looking around, and she noticed the big hotel.

"Beautiful hotel ka."

"Maybe we can stay there sometime."

"Oh, wery expensive, babe. Pang mahk, mahk ka."

"That's okay, Joy."

"Ka."

Tom marveled at the variety of traffic—long-tails, wooden junks, rowboats, ferries, jet skis, sailboats, houseboats, fishing boats, skiffs, rubber rafts, kayaks, and even a few yachts. He observed commercial barges hauling gravel, sand, and other construction materials. The condition of the boats indicated that their owners never thought about maintenance and didn't get into trouble for ignoring it.

Tom saw debris drifting past that resembled the sides of their boat. Joy stared at the river. The current, waves, and clumps of floating green plants interested her. They watched groups of all shapes of plastic bottles bobbing up and down, and congregating in eddies to perform their Sevillanas dances.

"Look that wittle island, babe. It move ka. Green ka."

"You could stand on it, but not me."

Joy → "He, he, he."

Tom → "Ha, ha, ha."

Joy looked confused. She didn't understand his joke. They laughed at that too.

While heading upstream into the current, their boat continued to sputter, making slow but steady progress. Rats darted in and about trash piles along the shore, occasionally taking a water route. Adjacent to the long-tail, frequent swirls showed that below its muddy surface, the river contained fish. The wiry, black whiskers belonged to catfish. Minnows escaped from their predators by going airborne. Joy enjoyed the ride.

Chapter 37

"You WANT SEE snake show?" the boat captain asked.

"Joy?"

"Okay. Me no chorp snake ka. Mai chorp ka."

"Sanuk."

"Ka."

"Okay, we go."

"Ka pom."

"Krap."

Wanting to get back on land, Joy agreed to the show. The driver motored noisily farther up and maneuvered to the river's edge. A teenage Thai boy ran down and grabbed the fraying rope that the captain tossed. The barefoot boy caught the rope, stuck it between his teeth, and pulled the narrow boat toward the crumbling dock.

Tom exited the unstable boat first. On the uneven dock, he spread his feet widely and shifted his weight back and forth.

"Give me your hand, baby."

"Ka."

"That's good. Easy."

"Ka."

Frightened about dying in the murky water, Joy reached up nervously. He balanced her.

"I've got you. Here … here you go, baby. Weeeee. Wow-weeee."

With one hand, he easily lifted her out.

"Weeeee. He, he, he."

"Okay?"

"Ka."

"That wasn't too bad, was it, baby?"

"Wery fun ka. You sweet, babe."

"Good, baby."

"Sanuk mahk ka."

Once out, and off the rickety dock, Joy sighed and wiped her hands.

The boy led them up decaying stairs and past a few vendors. They sold Buddhist amulets, small wooden carvings, antique-looking trinkets, boat models, pinwheels, buttons, bottle openers, 'I LOVE Thailand' stickers, kid's toys, paintings, postcards, pillows, earrings and jewelry, coins, ashtrays, cigarette lighters, stuffed animals, plastic snakes and dinosaurs, handbags, Thai snacks, bars of soap carved into lotus-flower designs, keychains, picture books of Bangkok, maps, phone covers, glasses, shells, magnets, selfie sticks, CDs, umbrellas, hats, T-shirts, traditional clothing, and more.

Thai music blared nearby. The unpleasant river odor from the raw sewage made Tom hurry. Another pair of hawkers sold steamed corn, fruit slices, rice wrapped in bamboo leaves, chips, coffee, tea, bottled water, and soft drinks. Tom followed the snake-show signs and led Joy by the hand through narrow pathways.

"You wery good, babe."

"Thanks, baby."

"Ka."

"Oops."

Because they made up the entire audience, the performance, beneath the moldy tarp, started as soon as they took their crumbling seats. An old Thai man with a crooked back emerged from a door behind the cracked-concrete platform. He carried a couple of heavy burlap bags. Tom noticed an uncanny resemblance to their boat driver, and assumed the two men were related. Joy didn't notice anything.

The bag's sides shot out randomly, as if being poked by a captured gnome. On the man's bare chest and stomach, Tom could see battle scars, from when cobras had moved faster. Tom hoped there was plenty of antidote within arm's reach. The thought of giving the fellow mouth-to-mouth repulsed Tom.

"I hope that he moves quickly today."

"Ka."

"Look at the art work."

"Him many tattoo, babe."

"I'll say."

"Me li-eh Froggy. Froggy wery cute ka."

Joy squeezed Tom's hand. He stared into her eyes.

"Thanks, baby."

"Ka."

Tom wondered where the snake charmer came from. How many times he had been bitten? If he ever almost died? If his son was going to take over the business? If the guy would get bitten today? How many shows there were per day? Joy for her part sat, watched, and waited for the real show to begin.

The snake charmer's unkempt hair, tattoos, wiry frame, bizarre demeanor, and piercing eyes entertained already, even without the snakes. His hand circled to unwrap the twine securing the top of a burlap bag. He flipped the bag upside down and dumped a 12-foot cobra onto the stage. It sat upright.

"Oh, no ka. Mai ka."

"Wow!"

"King cobra," the young Thai announcer stated, "Wery deadly."

"Ka."

"Where did he get that?"

"Thai wery many snake ka. Mai chorp ka."

"This should be interesting."

"Ka."

When viewed from the side, the forward part of the king cobra formed a capital L, and the remainder, a stabilizing figure eight. As the man backed away, he tossed the empty bag aside with great panache. The cobra stared. The other stage-side bag's frenzied activity increased. Joy squirmed in her seat. She gripped Tom's hand tightly.

"Babe, you look. Joy fraid ka."

"It's fine, baby. Don't worry. They can't reach you. I'm sure the guy knows what he's doing."

"Me not look ka. Him too old. Too slow ka."

"Don't worry, baby. Everything will turn out all right."

"Me no sure."

"Try to watch, okay?"

"Ka."

"Good, baby."

"Ka."

Tom settled her down. The cobra flared its hood, as the wiry man approached. The crackpot antagonized it.

"King-cobra boxing krap. Wery dangerous."

"Oh, oh."

"Are you kidding me?"

"King cobra."

"Ka."

"Look at that."

"Ka."

The charmer began poking at the agitated king cobra with his bare hands. As the drama unfolded, the attentive announcer turned up the music.

"King-cobra boxing. Too dangerous krap. Wery too dangerous."

"Ka. Me fraid ka."

"Don't worry, baby."

"Ka."

"Wery too dangerous krap."

The old man lunged forward, and the snake struck. He jumped backwards, just out of fangs' reach. The geezer sighed, having recovered from his mistake. Tom heard a thud. The young announcer accidently dropped the microphone.

"Oh. Mai ka. Mai."

"Shit. This guy's insane."

"Oh. Noooo."

"He may get bitten."

"Mai. Mai chorp ka."

"This is crazy, baby."

Joy bounded into Tom's lap.

"Joy no li-eh ka. Wery big snake ka."

She wiggled and kissed him and smiled.

CHAPTER 38

A S THE COBRA approached, the man circled. The snake tattoos on his back came into view. The agitated cobra remained center stage, rotating its head and slithering to face its nemesis. The two spectators maintained constant eyes on the old man.

After circling the giant snake, the geezer slapped at it. The snake lunged and missed his hand. Each time the charmer performed this maneuver, Joy gasped and clutched Tom more tightly. The scene intensified, as the old man took bigger risks. He hoped the bold actions would be rewarded with a large tip.

"King-cobra boxing. Don't try this at home krap. Take year to learn king-cobra boxing. Many year. Not too many cobra boxer left in Thailand krap. Many left us already krap. Wery dangerous krap. Wery dangerous. King-cobra boxing."

As if one cobra weren't enough, the guy dumped two smaller cobras from the other bag. The madman swung the burlap around his head in a wild display, and he tossed it aside. He jumped up and down. His yah bah pills kept him energized and fearless.

The three cobras reared up. They watched the familiar man. He slid side to side on the balls of his feet, hands dangling by his thighs. He pressed forward and slapped at them with an open hand—a quick left and right. The group of cobras struck. The man jumped backward.

"Nooo! Mai ka."

"I don't believe this guy."

"Ka. Him mai smart."

"The guy has lost his mind."

"Ka."

"Wery danger ka."

"King-cobra boxing krap."

Joy stood up and retreated. The man grabbed the smallest cobra by the tail and flung it back to center stage. It quickly resumed its upright position. The man sprang farther back. The cobra struck.

"Did you see that?"

"Ka."

"Cobra wrestling krap."

"The guy's insane."

"Wery, wery stupid ka."

"See that?"

"Ka. Me photo ka."

"Cobra MMA. Wery danger krap. Wery, wery danger. The big cobra him name Mike Tyson. The little jumping cobra there. Him name Mike Jordan.

The third cobra called ... um, the third cobra ... him Rambo. John J. Rambo krap. Wery danger krap. Him Mike Jordan ... oops."

"They have American names. The announcer's confused."

"Ka."

"Do cobras have ears? Can they hear?"

"Mai kow jai ka."

"Just wondering, baby."

"Ka."

"Wery danger krap."

"Uh, yeah."

"Ka."

The charmer grabbed the two smallest cobras by their tails. They arched around in an attempt to bite. He spun and released their tails just in the nick of time, tossing the snakes outward. The forgotten one jumped. The man moved quickly, but the big one faster. They applauded his reckless moves.

As the show continued, the wild man made daring gestures toward the cobras. He liked swinging two of them, relying on centrifugal force as his defense. He defied the odds, but his scars proved not always.

Many times, it looked as though the cobras beat him. At the last-possible second, the fearless charmer sprang backwards. He displayed courage. Joy kept her eyes open most of the time, and the show thrilled her. Tom enjoyed its novelty.

When the show concluded, after rehearsed remarks by the announcer, they gave the old fellow a long round of applause. The proud man bowed and walked over. Tom noticed a limp. The red welt on his leg confirmed a bite.

Tom handed the poor fellow 200 baht. He seemed pleased. The charmer disappeared quickly in search of antidote. Tom shook his head in disbelief. Joy's palms were sweaty.

On the way back, Tom bought a cha yen. The ice-filled cup contained little tea. When they reached the dock, the driver was ready to continue. Tom stabilized Joy, as she entered the wobbly boat. Once comfortably sitting down, he released his grip.

"Crazy old man."

"Ka. Wery crazy."

"I wouldn't be playing that game."

"Ka."

"You know I think that he may have even gotten bitten. I saw him limping badly at the end. Then he quickly disappeared. Do you think he was bitten?"

"Ka."

"Did you understand me?"

"Ka."

Tom smiled, and Joy smiled back. Tom doubted her comprehension. She just nodded and replied 'ka.' They laughed.

Tom handed the escort a generous tip. The boy grinned, and it was only then that Tom realized how rotten the young boy's teeth are. His only water comes from the river. Even if the poor boy does own a toothbrush, it is obvious that he doesn't have access to toothpaste. Tom felt badly. Joy didn't notice anything unusual. He positioned himself behind her, as before.

The captain had started the boat's poopy engine already. The boy tossed back the worn line. Using his bare foot, he gave them a firm push away from the dock.

"Thanks."

"Krap."

"Ka."

"Bye."

"Korp khun krap."

The couple waved. He waved back and went out of view, as they turned upstream. Only then did it occur to Tom that Joy and the boy are about the same age. The boy seemed very young.

"That man wery stupid."

"Yeah, I wouldn't do that for a million bucks."

"Joy no li-eh cobra. Mai chorp ka."

"Chorp."

"Babe, you speak Thai wery well."

"Korp khun krap."

"Ka."

Joy felt pleased that Tom picked up the Thai language. As they traveled farther up the river, the traffic decreased. The river became calmer. Joy relaxed. While puffing away on a cigarette, their driver steered the boat with his leg. They went under the King Rama I Memorial Bridge.

Chapter 39

THE NEXT STOP was Wat Arun—one of the most famous temples in Thailand.

As the temple appeared, Tom declared, "That's Wat Arun."

"Weally? You smart man, babe."

"Yeah, I read about it."

"Ka."

Tom's rudimentary knowledge of Bangkok impressed the little Issarn girl. Joy spent her time at the massage parlor and had seen nothing in the city. The driver brought them to the side of the river. This time, she exited the boat easily.

"See-sip haa natee krap."

"Ka." Joy took Tom's hand. "We came back forty-five minute ka."

"Okay."

Tom checked his watch. At the temple's impressive entrance, several vendors sold lottery tickets. A group of Thais stood there discussing numbers. They believe temples bring good luck. Strong incense filled the air. The towering Wat Arun tapers, as it reaches toward the sky. It is the tallest temple she has seen.

Tom snapped pictures for Joy and avoided getting his taken. Whenever he took her picture, Joy smiled beautifully. They walked around the grounds. At one place, they removed their shoes to enter a building. The hot stones almost burned his feet. Displays of gold Buddhas fill the rooms.

In front of one large Buddha, Joy joined others, getting down on her knees and prostrating three times. An orange-robed monk sat in one corner. While chanting in the ancient Pali language, he blessed worshippers. He threw water on them from a bundle of sticks that he dipped into a holy vat. When the splash hit the bowing patrons, they shook and scooted backward on their knees. Once far enough away, they rose to their feet, feeling renewed.

Sitting at a table, another monk chanted. He wrapped a thick, white twine around a worshipper's wrist and tied the twine in a knot. The monk trimmed the loose ends with a pair of scissors, before moving on to the next in line.

After marveling at antique gold objects in the temple, they headed out. Tom dropped a 50-baht bill into one of the glass collection boxes, and Joy did the same with a bill Tom gave her. She never had given money away before, except to someone in her family. Joy stared at the pile of cash in the clear box. They found their shoes among the hot pile out front.

Time flew by during the temple visit, and they hurried back to the long-tail boat. It wasn't too much farther up the Chao Phraya River, until they could see the Grand Palace Complex. Tom originally planned to go there to see the famous Emerald Buddha, the King's palace, and the temple buildings, but time escaped. Perhaps when he came back, they would go.

Using Joy's phone, Tom snapped a few photos of her with the Grand Palace in the background.

"Wery beautiful, babe. Joy chorp mahk ka."

"Yes, so big and beautiful. Lots of gold. The tile is amazing too."

"Wery pretty ka. Mee khwam suk ka."

"We go next time."

"Ka."

Joy's carefree manner makes being around her easy and fun. He loves her simplicity. She doesn't put up any walls. They traveled farther up river to the Tha Phra Chan Ferry stop. A number of white egrets stood on a concrete wall. A few of the skittish ones took to the air.

"Babe, look ka."

"So beautiful."

"Nok white. Surin no have ka."

"We call them egrets in English."

"E grits?"

"Yeah, that's right."

"You wery smart man ka."

"Thanks, baby."

"Ka."

Tropical vegetation covers the wall. Tom could see fish swirls in the brown-colored water. The motionless egrets waited poised to make a catch.

"Boat turn here krap."

"Ka."

"Okay."

"Babe, we back ka. Finish ka."

"Okay. Too bad we didn't have more time. I like it out here."

"Ka. Sanuk mahk ka."

"Yeah, this is great."

"Ka."

The driver managed a U-turn by swinging the rusty pipe in a wide arch. Throughout the motion, he balanced a cigarette in his chapped lips. The trio headed back down river. Their speed increased noticeably with the favorable current. The waves splashing against the boat no longer worried Joy. She kept both hands on top of Tom's.

Even though the sun sank toward the horizon, Bangkok's high humidity kept them uncomfortably warm. They welcomed the occasional splash.

"Wery fast boat ka."

"Yes. We're going downstream."

"Ka."

Although she didn't understand, Joy responded by reflex. Her long hair tickled his face. Everything was new to Joy. No matter what they saw, she enjoyed it. When she didn't understand something, she didn't feel inferior. He made her comfortable.

Tom felt great being with the sexy little Thai girl. Many questions popped into his head about her, but he chose not to ask. If she wanted to tell him more, she would. He keeps many secrets that he never can share with anyone. Luckily, she isn't curious. This aspect of Joy's personality makes him feel very comfortable.

As the boat made its way back toward the pier, the river traffic increased. A couple times, they brushed up against boat taxis. Tom warned to keep her hands inside. Their driver puffed constantly on a cigarette, but remained alert.

Tipping a long-tail boat over is easy, especially when turning or getting jostled by a wave from a larger vessel. As they returned, setting foot on land again made them smile. Tom tipped the driver.

"Korp khun krap."

"How did you like that, baby?"

"Wery good, babe. Chorp mahk ka. Sanuk mahk ka."

"Sanuk?" Tom finally asked what the word meant.

"Sanuk mean 'fun' ka."

"Okay. Sanuk mahk krap. Me too. Good view of Bangkok from the water."

"Joy never boat before. Chorp. Chorp mahk ka."

"Sanuk krap. You did great."

"Ka. Me feel funny ka."

"Probably your equilibrium. It's off from the waves."

"Equi ... brie ...?"

"That feeling will be gone soon, baby."

"Ka."

CHAPTER 40

THE NAVY SEAL checked his watch. They had time to walk around. He decided to buy Joy a gift at one of the jewelry shops. He led her away from the hustle-and-bustle of the BTS metro area and the pier at Saphan Taksin. The mingling crowd had continued to build throughout the day. After a short walk among the masses, they arrived in Chinatown in the Samphanthawong District.

I'm into file JoyPart34 now, and there is only one remaining. Tom missed an earlier chance to propose to Joy. He might purchase a ring in Chinatown. I'm sure she would love to get engaged before he moves to Chiang Mai. I continue.

Street vendors peddled their wares on the web of Bangkok's sois. Tom noticed the customers in the noodle shops picked up huge quantities with their chopsticks and slurped, before spitting half back into their bowls. Joy noticed the gold shops. She never asked for anything, but he could see her staring into every shop. The poor Issarn girl marveled at the hanging gold chains, while he admired the mature saleswomen in red dresses.

Although the attractive couple turned many heads, they ignored the attention. When women and gay men asked to take his picture, Tom turned them down. His refusal to accept their flattery brought Joy closer. She felt proud to be with the handsome American. She loved his attitude.

"Want to look in a gold shop, baby?"

"Pang mahk, babe. Okay ka."

"This one looks interesting."

"Ka."

"Come on."

Tom led Joy into the shop. A polite and attractive Chinese-Thai saleswoman in a form-fitting red dress approached them. Given Tom's strong attraction to her, he changed his mind about purchasing an engagement ring. If he can't be faithful to Joy, it's better to wait. Many buddies ended up divorced due to infidelity.

Tom decided to look at gold bracelets. The impecunious girl reluctantly tried on a number of different ones. She worried she might steal one. Joy became more at ease with the clerk's assistance and compliments. Joy adapted to seeing the precious metal on her wrist, and the prices no longer troubled her. She controlled her fears.

Joy never realized he changed his mind about buying a ring. He felt better about having delayed the purchase and proposal.

"Do you have any anklets? Chains for the ankle?"

"Ankle?"

"Yes. Here."

He pointed at Joy's ankle.

"Kow jai ka. Mee ka."

"Her have."

"Okay, let's take a look. See what she has."

"Ka."

The clerk motioned them to a different section. She brought out several anklets. Tom enjoyed watching her place them on Joy. The woman's long fingernails facilitated opening the tiny clasps. He preferred the chain, with small charm hearts, that fit on top of Joy's ankle bone.

"Is this twenty-four carat?"

"Yes, Mister. Come with paper ka."

"You like this one, Joy?"

"Sooay mahk, mahk. Tow rai ka?"

Joy discussed the price. He watched and listened, as they went back and forth. After the discussion, Joy seemed disappointed.

"Babe, this one pang mahk ka. Pang gern bpai."

"How much, baby?"

"She say last price thirty-thousand ka."

"Oh. Hmm."

"Mister, normal price thirty-five thousand. Special price for you ka."

"That's your best price?"

"Mister, boss won't sell less."

"That she final price."

"Um, I see."

"Ka."

"Without heart not expensive. Me have other, Mister."

The deliberating American looked at Joy, the lovely saleswoman, back at his girlfriend, and then the saleswoman again. He knew Joy would love to have the anklet. It weighed over half an ounce. He hesitated. Bangkok nudged him—you can't take it with you when you die. The ring would have cost him much more. He could tell how happy Joy would be if he brought it. She waited nervously.

"Okay, Joy. I want to buy it for you."

Joy hands covered her mouth. Gold usually retains its value and can be resold easily in Thailand. It symbolizes wealth; it's like cash. The gift impressed her. In a gross violation of Thai culture, she kissed him. It was a deep kiss.

"Joy love you wery much, babe. You good man ka."

"You're so special, baby."

"Nee sooay mahk, mahk ka. Pang dooay. Expensive ka."

"You're welcome, baby. I like little hearts."

"Mee khwam suk ka. Mee khwam suk mahk."

"Good, baby. It looks lovely on you."

"Ka."

The three moved to another area to complete the transaction. He counted out thirty 1,000-baht notes and handed them to the cashier. While she carefully re-counted, Joy clutched his arm. She couldn't believe that she would own gold.

When he handed the receipt and the certificate of authentication to Joy, she realized that the gold is hers. It was one of the happiest moments of her life. The cashier put the precious anklet in a red-velvet box and tied it shut with a piece of gold ribbon. Tom smiled.

"Korp khun ka."

"Thank you."

"Come back and see me ka. My name Ying."

"Okay."

"Joy not wear on street ka."

"Good idea, baby."

"Ka."

"Good-bye and thank you, Ying."

"Good-bye ka. Hope to see you again …"

"Good-bye."

"Bye ka."

Joy placed the anklet in her handbag. They embraced; she smiled. She just became one of the wealthiest people in her village. Other girls would be jealous. They would want to know about her rich American boyfriend, and if he had any friends.

"Joy love you, babe. Love you too much ka."

Tom held back the words that were on the tip of his tongue. He loves Joy a great deal. But, Bangkok threw other beautiful women at him. He felt it prudent to wait before proposing.

"You're wonderful and very important to me, Joy. I'm so happy with you."

"Me wery happy. Me have gold ka."

"Yes, you have gold."

"Ankle. Sooay mahk ka. Korp khun ka. Pang mahk."

"You're welcome, baby."

"Babe, you good man ka. Wery sweet. I love you ka."

"Thanks, baby. You're the best."

"Ka."

Joy squeezed his hand. She didn't want to let go. She never owned anything this expensive. The anklet cost as much as a motorcycle. Her beaming smile revealed a passionate love. For people in Issarn, receiving an expensive gift carried a significant meaning—relating to loyalty. They believe in karma and luck. Joy's luck changed for the better. Her life was going so well now. She thought of leaving Lucky Massage behind.

Tom wanted to kiss Joy, but he respected the culture and refrained. Her great happiness almost forced the words, 'I love you,' to emerge from his lips. Somehow, he restrained himself. They stared in each other's eyes and smiled. For a brief moment, Bangkok allowed them some peace.

When Tom reached a hand into his pocket, his notes from earlier in the day brought him back to reality. He pulled out the paper and looked at their schedule. Due to time constraints, they skipped the Jim Thompson House too. They jumped ahead on the schedule to the Vertigo Bar at the Banyan Tree Hotel.

Tom decided if things felt right, he would go ahead and propose there. If he wasn't sure, he would wait. Joy loved being with him. Although he would be leaving the next day, she wanted to have fun this evening. The gold anklet made her feel secure in their relationship.

Chapter 41

I OPEN THE LAST file. I realize now I won't have the time to go back and make additional edits. I'll try to get the manuscript to a copyeditor for review before I send it to my friend, Adrian. The coronavirus pandemic has thrown a monkey wrench into many plans. The tragic death of my father consumes me. I never anticipated I would lose Dad this year.

I sit down with a bottle of Maker's Mark. I pour myself a half glass and drink it. I refill. I'm going to finish the story now. I don't plan on getting up until it's done. "Whichever way you decide, good luck, ole boy."

After the ride in Bangkok's heavy traffic, they arrived at the five-star Banyan Tree Hotel. The green space in front creates a small oasis among the city's cranes, pollution, and jumble of wires. Just as the floating islands on the Chao Praya River connect one to nature, this artificial niche, entered immediately after exiting Bangkok's concrete jungle, puts patrons into a pleasant mood. As Joy pulled herself out of the taxi, Tom tipped the driver.

"Korp khun krap."

"Ka pom."

"Chok dee krap."

"Ka pom."

The couple headed to the Vertigo Bar on the 60th floor of the narrow skyscraper.

"Baby, let's take the stairs."

"You joke me?"

"Yes, baby … I'm joking."

"He, he, he. Joy no walk. Take lift ka."

"Sure, baby."

"Babe, you funny."

"Just teasing you, baby."

"Ka."

A well-groomed attendant pushed the button to summon the lift. Tom watched the numbers count down quickly.

"Look, wery fast ka."

"Yeah. It's 60 floors."

"Wow. Wery tall ka."

"Yeah, it's one of the tallest buildings in Bangkok. Should be a good view. Maybe cooler up there."

"Ka."

"Here, sir," the attendant pointed.

"Thanks."

"Ka."

The silver doors opened. A white-haired farang exited the lift with a beautiful Thai woman hanging off his arm. She appeared drunk and wobbled in her stilettos. The farang smiled knowingly at Tom. He smiled back. As the drunk woman waved good-bye, they entered the elevator. Tom instinctively glanced at the security camera. It's a system he could easily defeat.

"Vertigo."

"Yes, sir."

"Here we go."

"Weeeee. Wery fast ka."

"I guess one of the fastest lifts in Thailand?"

"Ka pom."

"Weeeee."

As the lift accelerated to maximum speed, Joy sensed herself being pushed down, and she grabbed the American's hand. He noticed on the panel, floors 51 and 54 were omitted. Private floors, he wondered.

Their ears popped. Joy experienced a whirling sensation and loss of balance. She became giddy. When they climbed the final flight of stairs to reach the bar, she relied on him for balance.

"Joy feel funny ka. He, he, he."

"You're experiencing vertigo."

"Wer ... wert ... I go."

"Yes, vertigo. A dizzy feeling—you lose your balance. That's the name of the bar."

"Oh, weally. He, he, he. Wert ... go. He, he."

"They gave it the right name."

"Good wiew, wery good wiew ka."

"Yes, excellent."

"Me feel strange. Dizzy ka."

"You'll be okay, baby. Here. Windy."

"Me strange ka."

While watching Joy's blowing hair, he squeezed her hand. She maintained balance.

"Cooler up here. Much nicer."

"Don't wook down. Wery high ka."

"It's fine, baby. Don't worry, baby."

Tom detected a sway in the building.

"Joy dizzy ka."

She steadied herself on his powerful arm.

"Let's sit down, baby. You'll feel better."

"Ka. He, he, he."

Tom couldn't help but think of a paralyzed Jimmy Stewart, suffering from a spinning head in Hitchcock's Vertigo. With his flight scheduled for early morning, he knew his time in Bangkok with Joy was ending. He became sentimental. She didn't notice his mood change.

A waiter approached.

"There?"

"Ka pom."

While enjoying the views of illuminated Bangkok, they celebrated their relationship. At 60 floors high, the separation sanitized the salacious city below. Bangkok's tentacles couldn't reach them. In some strange way, Tom knew he would miss Bangkok. The city didn't let go easily.

At the bar, the clientele consisted entirely of couples—always an old farang paired with a well-dressed Thai woman. Tom and Joy were under-dressed compared to everyone else, as they arrived straight from their tour. Many ladies assumed he isn't as rich as their older farang boyfriends. Joy didn't notice.

Tom ordered drinks, and together they chose appetizers. Before too long, she adapted to the building's height, and her vertigo dissipated. She walked to the skyscraper's edge and stared down. He pointed out where they'd gone. Joy couldn't understand their route. She felt thrilled to recognize several landmarks though.

They enjoyed their drinks and plush seats. Joy wanted to get a buzz. She didn't want to think about her boyfriend's departure. Tom noticed that many came for just one drink and to snap a few pictures. After several rounds, he called for the check.

Tom felt good about things, as did Joy. The alcohol added to her high. She lives carefree and in the moment. A problem is something to solve only if it becomes a disaster, impending disasters don't yet require attention. She would worry about tomorrow, tomorrow, if ever.

In the morning, Tom expected a difficult goodbye. He thought that he would propose to Joy then. But, for now at least, he wanted to live as she taught him, worry free. He didn't overthink things, as they left for their final night.

I save the file and shutdown Windows. I rub my hands together and pick up my glass of Maker's Mark. I stagger

over to the window and press my face against the glass. I stare
out at the hazy Naval Academy's Chapel ...

THAI TO ENGLISH DICTIONARY

A

angrit *English*
aow *to want*
arai *what*
aroy *delicious*

B

baan *house*
boom, boom *slang for sexual intercourse*
bpak *mouth*
bplah meuk *octopus*

C

cha nom yen *Thai milk tea*
cha yen *ice tea*
chah *slow*
chah chah *slowly*
cheu *name*
chok dee *good luck*
chooay dooay *help*
chorp *like*

D

dai *can*

daeng *red*
dee *good*
dee gwah *good or better*
di chan *polite way of saying 'me' (female)*
doi *mountain*
dooay *also*

G

gai *chicken*
gai yaang khao neeaw *grilled chicken with sticky rice*
geek *a girlfriend who receives large amounts of financial support, usually in return for sexual favors*
geng *smart*
gern *a lot*
glang *middle*

H

haa *five*
huay *stream*

J

jing jing *really*
joop *kiss*
joop, joop *kisses*

K

ka *polite female ending word*
kaew *glass*
kem *salty*
khao ka moo *pork with rice*

khao neeaw ma muang *yellow mango with sticky rice*

khun *you*

khwam suk *happiness or feeling of happiness*

kitteung *miss*

koh *island*

koo muang *moat*

korp khun *thank you*

kor-toht *excuse me*

kow jai *understand*

kow jai mai *do you understand*

kow dtom *rice soup*

krang *times, as in an expression such as 'two times'*

krap *polite male ending word*

kwah *right*

kway teaw ladna *stir-fried rice noodles*

L

lor *handsome*

lor mahk *very handsome*

luk *child*

M

mahk *a lot or very*

mai *no*

mai kow jai *don't understand*

manow *lemon*

mee *to have*

mee khwam suk *to be happy or to have happiness*

meu *hand*

moo dat deo *dried pork*

N

naka *a deeper meaning polite-ending word, expressing more than ka*

nam bplow *drinking water*

nam-dtahn *sugar*

nang *movie*

natee *minute (referring to time)*

nee *this*

neeaw *sticky*

neung *one*

nid noi *little*

nok *bird*

nong *used to refer to a younger brother*

P

pahsah *language*

pan *thousand*

pang *expensive*

pom *I or sir*

poot *speak*

prick kee noo *Thai chilies*

R

reo *fast*

ruea *boat*

S

sahm *three*

sahm sip *thirty*
sahy *left*
sanuk *fun*
saphan *bridge*
see *four*
set *to finish or to orgasm*
sip *ten*
som tam *papaya salad*
som-o *pomelo*
sooay *beautiful*
sorng *two*

T

tam mai *why*
tee-rak *sweetheart*
tom yum goong *hot and sour spicy soup with shrimp*
turagit *business*

U

uan *fat*

V

veena *moon*

W

waan *ring*
wan *sweet*

Y

yah bah *a mixture of methamphetamine and caffeine*

yai *large*
yeen *jeans*
Yippon *Japan*
yut *stop*

THE THAI WIFE
SERIES OF NOVELS

THE MAIN NARRATOR is a Nobel laureate in literature, awarded for his writings about Thailand. He discovers unfinished novels in his apartment in Annapolis, Maryland. As he begins to edit, bringing them to the Nobel level, the coronavirus pandemic strikes. It wreaks havoc on his family. While dealing with personal issues, including numerous affairs, the Nobel laureate relays the story of Doctor Adventure.

Doc is a decorated Navy SEAL and cybersecurity expert. His polyorchidism results in an unusually high testosterone level. His intensity leads to questionable behavior in the field, and Doc is fired from the National Security Agency. He continues covert operations in Thailand, as a critical but underground asset. He conducts cyber operations against the Chinese. His cover involves exploring Thailand's massage parlors and bars.

Doc falls in love with a series of gorgeous Thai ladies. Each time that he is about to pop the big question, disaster strikes. He continues his quest for finding the perfect Thai wife through dozens of intense encounters. He meets several ladyboys, and his own sexuality is called into question.

Completed in the Thai Wife Series of Novels

The Thai Wife Story Joy (Book 1)

The Thai Wife Story Star (Book 2)

Planned

The Thai Wife Story Sugar (Book 3)

The Thai Wife Story Gun (Book 4)

The Thai Wife Story Patty (Book 5)

The Thai Wife Story Opal (Book 6)

The Thai Wife Story Apple (Book 7)

The Thai Wife Story Peach (Book 8)

The Thai Wife Story Moon (Book 9)

The Thai Wife Story Ying (Book 10)

THE THAI WIFE STORY STAR: PREVIEW

THE FOLLOWING IS a preview of the first chapter of the novel *The Thai Wife Story Star*. The actual version of chapter one may differ.

CHAPTER 1
(Preview of *The Thai Wife Story Star*)

I EMPATHIZE WITH the young Issarn girl, Joy, and I hope the Navy SEAL, Tom, will return to Bangkok to see his masseuse soon. Before he departed for Chiang Mai, I felt sure he would propose marriage. I thought he purchased a ring. I hope she's okay, and doesn't do anything foolish.

I don't have much time to work on the novels, as Cam-Tu is arriving for dinner. My Vietnamese lover is bringing vegetarian spring rolls. I'll provide Maker's Mark, which she refers to as Mark Make. Before CT arrives, I want to see how Tom's flight goes.

I navigate to the Star folder. The situation is similar to the Joy folder. There are three-dozen files. I open the file Part1 Star. As a Nobel laureate in literature, I edit on the fly.

The Navy SEAL sat at his gate in Bangkok's Suvarnabhumi International Airport, waiting for the boarding announcement from Thai Airways. The gate area, teeming with farangs and Chinese tourists, offered limited seating to those just arriving. While ripping the limbs off a stuffed animal, Chinese kids ran around a Samsung monitor in front of the American. They shouted for their parents' attention. The adults never looked up from their mobiles. The kids continued shouting. Only a couple dozen Thais were bound for Chiang Mai.

Tourists examined copies of Lonely Planet's *Thailand*. Monks in orange robes and Birkenstocks relaxed in reserved seats, and played with iPhones. A group of sunburned, long-haired backpackers in tie-dyed T-shirts stretched out on the dusty floor. Staff checked passports and tore boarding passes in half. Broken English translations followed each Thai announcement. Despite the distractions, Tom reflected.

When the American kissed his little Issarn girl good-bye, tears flowed freely from her eyes and ran into his mouth. At her final words of 'Love you ka' and a wave, an unpleasant feeling of separation lodged in his stomach. He missed her. Tom second guessed himself about not proposing.

I knew he would regret that. I keep reading, and editing.

The poor Thai girl missed her American boyfriend. She felt like a failure. While Tom sat alone at

Suvarnabhumi, she cried in a corner of Lucky Massage. They planned to text and talk. Their agreement provided her little solace. She didn't know if she would ever see him again.

Tom took comfort in thinking he would meet Joy again soon. He'd been instructed to travel to Chiang Mai alone. If he'd had his way, she would have gone too. She wanted to go. Joy didn't understand why she couldn't. He couldn't explain.

Having dodged the kids and backpackers, at the jetway's entrance, Tom handed his boarding pass to a pretty Thai girl. She checked his ID.

"Welcome ka. Go ahead, sir."

"Thanks."

"Ka."

Tom reached the airplane near the front. Only monks were ahead. They fly business class for free on Thai Airways. The Navy SEAL trailed their orange robes.

"Sa waa dii ka. Welcome on board, sir."

"Welcome. Welcome."

"Thanks."

"Welcome ka. This way, sir."

"Okay. I've got it."

"Ka."

The overhead bin provided plenty of space, and Tom stored his bag. Once sitting comfortably in business class, he wiped off with a cool towel.

"Drink, sir?"

"I'll have a double Baileys on the rocks. Here."

The stewardess gripped the towelette in tongs. "Thank you ka."

Tom looked at the runway and stared in the direction of departing planes. Still lost in thought, he didn't see their shapes. His mind circled in a haze, and he longed for a drink of Joy's magic potion. The Baileys proved inadequate. His adorable Thai neighbor brought him down for a soft landing.

"Ha-low, MISter, my name Pan."

The lovely Issarn girl extended her delicate hand. He took it. She squeezed affectionately.

"Pan?"

"Ka."

"Good to meet you, Pan. I'm Doc."

"Doc? Li-eh doctor?"

"Yes, short for doctor."

"Oh, you big man ka. Important. Nice to meet you, Doc. You big blue eye ka."

I chuckle at the blue cyclops. Ole boy, Thais won't ever get plurals. I don't bother to correct this error.

"Thanks."

"You stay Chiang Mai?"

"Yes, I'm moving up there for a while."

"Me too. I work there."

"Where are you from, Pan?"

"Excuse me. Here you go, sir." The stewardess turned to Pan, "Khun aow arai ka?"

"Nam bplow ka."

"Ka."

"I order water ka. I Si Saket, in Northeast Thailand. Me Issarn girl. I back Osaka, Yippon. Where you from?"

Although Pan hails from a poor farming family, her boyfriend is a rich, retired Japanese man. He bought her business-class tickets to and from Japan. She visits twice a year. When the weather turns cold, she returns. Pan works at My Tee-Rak Bar. Her generous allowance allows her to maintain a comfortable lifestyle. She even sends money home to family. They rely on her.

"I'm from America. Your English is excellent."

"You America man? America man good ka. I study English school."

Pan withheld that her boyfriend speaks English.

"Yes, I'm American. I like your hair."

"Thank you ka," she blushed.

"Sure. You're very beautiful."

"Korp khun ka."

"Krap."

"You can speak Thai?"

"Poot pahsah Thai dai nid noy krap."

They smiled. Pan's hair framed her round eyes. Two coils dropped down from its beehive-styled top. They resemble asps. Her boyfriend paid for the expensive hairdo, her implants, and surgery to round her almond-shaped eyes.

Tom guessed Pan was twentyish. Her big brown eyes and curvaceous body attract him. Her business-class ticket led Tom to surmise that she has a sugar daddy in Japan.

"Would you li-eh more drink, sir?"

"Yeah, sure. Another double. Same. Baileys. Here you go."

"Ka. Ka."

"Thanks."

When the stewardess turned away, Pan whispered, "She ladyboy ka. Her man."

"What? Noooo way."

"Ka, she ladyboy."

"You're kidding me? I never would have known. Never in a million years. Thanks."

"Ka. She ladyboy."

"You absolutely sure?"

"Ka."

While revealing the ladyboy's secret, Pan's proximity and breath on Tom's ear, as well as her saying the libertine word 'ladyboy,' aroused him. He hasn't come to terms with his feelings toward ladyboys. In the military, he learned the don't ask, don't tell rule, but many of those who are attracted to the same sex suffer from guilty feelings.

A feeling of shame from being captivated by the ladyboy wreaked havoc on Tom's emotions. As a hard man, one with advanced training in situational awareness, the ease with which he'd been duped troubled him. It was more than that though, much more. He adjusted himself in his seat.

Pan leaned toward Tom. She placed her hand on his arm. Her lips neared his ear again.

"Ladyboy man who dress and act li-eh woman. Wery beautiful ka. Male hormone mean firm shape. They tall li-eh model. Thailand good plastic surgeon. Ladyboy breast implant, nose job, hand, and more ka."

"Oh. Really?"

"Ka."

Tom touched his forehead. She touched his Adam's apple.

"A few surgery here. Then, her female voice too."

She pointed at his crotch.

"A few surgery there. Now woman stuff. Those with big organ keep it. Me sure she wery big."

"Oh, my. Really?"

"Ka."

Pan blushed. He fought against his smile, but lost. He shook his head. She twirled her fingers through her dangling hair. First, she coiled the hanging serpent, while covering up her long, red nails. Slowly, she released the ophidian, and set the curl and nails free. The two asps stared at him.

"Farang can't tell ladyboy from weal woman."

"Farang means foreigner, right?"

Tom put air quotes around 'foreigner.'

"Ka."

"She fooled me. Ha, ha, ha."

"Her fool all farang easy. Wery hot lady."

"Amazing Thailand."

"Ka. Wery amazin'."

"Hmm."

Pan's smile revealed a perfect set of white and straight teeth. She detected a change in his attitude toward the stewardess. She sensed his discomfort. Pan knows that some farang men find ladyboys irresistible, while others dislike them intensely. He seemed to be the former.

Their stewardess stands five seven, and with heels, five eleven. Whenever she walked through the cabin, Tom admired her. She's only a few inches shorter than him. Her pretty face rests on a long neck, and the red lipstick increased the size of her mouth. Her feminine demeanor and appearance tricked him completely. He couldn't believe she's a biological male. Tom sipped his creamy Baileys. He thought about Bpee.

I hear Cam-Tu. I want to be with her. I'll hold my Vietnamese lover extra tightly this evening.

BOOKS BY
RAYMOND GREENLAW

The Thai Wife Story Joy (also available in electronic form), Book 1 of *The Thai Wife Series of Novels.*

The Thai Wife Story Star (also available in electronic form), Book 2 of *The Thai Wife Series of Novels.*

Palmarès (also available in electronic form).

Raymond's Checklist for Traveling in the USA (also available in electronic form), Book 1 of *Raymond's Checklist Series.*

Raymond's Checklist for Traveling in Thailand (also available in electronic form), Book 2 of *Raymond's Checklist Series.*

Raymond's Checklist for Traveling the World (also available in electronic form), Book 3 of *Raymond's Checklist Series.*

Raymond's Checklist for His Personal Bucket List (also available in electronic form), Book 4 of *Raymond's Checklist Series.*

Raymond's Checklist for Gear for a Long Hike (also available in electronic form), Book 5 of *Raymond's Checklist Series.*

Raymond's Checklist Cycling Gear (also available in paperback form), Book 6 of *Raymond's Checklist Series*.

The Hazards of Cycling in Thailand: Guidelines for Tourists (also available in electronic form).

Trapped in Thailand's Cave (also available in electronic form).

The Pacific Crest Trail: Its Fastest Hike, second edition (also available in electronic form).

Bob: My Dad, the Fisherman: A Father and Son's Relationship (also available in electronic form).

(with Saowaluk Rattanaudomsawat) *Essential Conversational Thai: Learn to Speak Thai Quickly, while Traveling in Thailand*.

You'll Never Walk Alone: Love Poems for My Sweetheart (also available in electronic form).

Poems of Raymond Greenlaw, 1986–2005 (also available in electronic form).

The Fastest Hike across Thailand (expected October 2021).

About the Author

RAYMOND "WALL" Greenlaw was born in Providence, Rhode Island, USA to Roxy and Bob. Raymond has always enjoyed nature, big trees, lakes, mountains, and the sea. He writes about a wide range of topics and is the author of over 35 books.